SOLD TO MY EX'S DAD

AN AGE GAP, SECRET BABY ROMANCE

K.C. CROWNE

Copyright © 2024 by K.C. Crowne

All rights reserved.

No part of this book may be reproduced in any form or by any electronic or mechanical means, including information storage and retrieval systems, without written permission from the author, except for the use of brief quotations in a book review.

DESCRIPTION

Under the bright lights of a charity auction, my heart races...
Then I see HIM—a suave, enigmatic older man who doesn't just watch me—*he sees me*.
He wins a date with me for a staggering $25,000.

That night my mysterious bidder had me wanting to do things I'd never admit.
And I did them willingly, secure in the thought a one-time fling wouldn't come back to bit me.

I couldn't have been more wrong.

When we meet again, the stakes are much higher.
He's not only my new boss but also the father of my ex- a man still infatuated with me.

And now, as I clutch a positive pregnancy test...
I realize he's bound to become much more than a complicated fling.
How do you drop the bomb on a man who doesn't want more kids that he's about to be a dad again? *Surprise!*

Readers note: This is full-length standalone, older man, surprise pregnancy, ex's dad romance. You'll need a cool glass of water because the HEAT level is scorching. K.C. Crowne is an Amazon Top 8 Bestseller and International Bestselling Author.

CHAPTER 1

ALLIE

"Easy, tiger! Looks like you're ready to run like hell."

Under the harsh backstage lights of the charity auction, my heart races a mile a minute.

"I'd honestly rather be anywhere else right now," I confess, feeling the pressure.

Somehow, this spirited sous chef has ended up on the menu as tonight's main course.

"Remember, Al, it's for the kids," Stacy reminds me, her enthusiasm undiminished by her insane mermaid costume. Stacy reminds me, her voice brimming with excitement. The temptation to douse her with a bucket of toilet water for dragging me into this is overwhelming, but I resist.

I can't stay mad; the night's efforts are for a noble cause. The proceeds are set to benefit foster kids—a community I hold close, being a former foster kid myself. This thought soothes the chaotic butterflies in my stomach.

Still, the prospect of dating—especially auctioned off for charity—is as appealing as pulling my lashes out.

Peeking from behind the curtain, I survey the crowd. A sea of eager faces, all potential bidders.

I find myself questioning their motives. "Are they really here for the kids or to watch the spectacle?"

"Don't be like that. After all, this could be the start of something new," Stacy whispers, giving me a hopeful nudge.

"Okay Ariel on steroids, don't tell me you're hinting at a love connection tonight."

She shrugs. "You never know. Could be a cute story to tell your grandkids one day."

Her optimism is hard to escape, and despite the absurdity of the situation, I find myself begrudgingly intrigued.

Who knows what tonight might bring? Maybe I'll meet someone who isn't put off by a woman who knows her way around a chef's knife. Or, at the very least, someone who doesn't think microwaving pizza rolls counts as gourmet cooking.

"I look ridiculous," I mutter, tugging at the edges of my coveralls as if they might magically transform into something more me.

Stacy, however, dismisses my self-deprecation with a scoff, her eyes sweeping over my outfit as she tilts her head thoughtfully. "Please, you look incredible—seriously, it's a subtle kind of sexy," she insists confidently.

She has a way of boosting my confidence, even when I'm dressed for a mechanic's convention rather than a date.

Skeptically, I step in front of a nearby mirror for a once-over.

The auction's theme tonight is "Adventure Awaits," and my date, should someone actually bid on me, consists of a helicopter tour of NYC, hence the coveralls, the top part undone and tied around my waist, revealing a tight, white tank underneath. The outfit is meant to scream adventurous, I suppose, but all I'm hearing is a faint whimper of fashion distress.

Stacy catches my eye in the mirror; she's grinning at me mischievously.

"I'm a little jealous, actually. A helicopter ride over the city? Come on, that's bucket list material." Her outfit, with a shimmering tail fin to boot, is more suited to her destination.

"Yeah, well, your date at the aquarium sounds a hell of a lot more my speed," I quip, trying to smooth down my hair, which seems to have taken the adventure theme as a personal challenge. "Honestly, I'm starting to remember why I spend 90 percent of my waking hours in a kitchen, hidden away from people."

"That's precisely why it's so great you're here," Stacy insists, her voice firm but friendly. "You can't hide behind those pots and pans forever, Al. Besides, think of the stories you'll have for the next family meal."

I can't help but laugh, the sound echoing off the walls of our makeshift dressing room. She's right, of course. The kitchen is my comfort zone, my sanctuary from the unpredictability of the world outside. But standing there, poised on the brink of something completely out of my comfort zone, I feel a flicker akin to excitement—or maybe it's just the adrenaline from imminent public embarrassment.

As we make our way toward the stage, the reality of the situation settles in. I'm about to be auctioned off for a helicopter tour over one of the most iconic cities in the world, dressed like I'm about to repair the chopper rather than ride in it.

Just as Stacy and I are about to make our grand entrance to the world of auctioned dates, a guy strides off stage, his outfit screaming Broadway's *The Lion King* louder than a roar in the savanna. His face is lit up with a mix of shock and excitement as he heads straight for us, eager to share his disbelief with somebody.

"You won't believe the bid for my date!" he exclaims, barely containing his energy. "Outrageous!" He looks like he might burst into a rendition of "Circle of Life" at any moment.

Right on his heels, a girl glides past, her figure skater costume complete with faux ice skates slung over her shoulder. "If you think that's something," she says, catching bits of our impromptu huddle, "the bid for Rockefeller Center ice skating was through the roof!"

Stacy claps her hands in delight. "This is amazing! It's all going to such a good cause."

I'm about to agree when a snippet of conversation from behind us catches my ear. I casually turn and glimpse another date for the evening, decked out in what I can only assume is her best attempt at a Cinderella gown. She's giggling with her friend. "I just hope I find Mr. Right tonight," she says, a twinkle in her eye.

Her friend, dressed in a costume that's a cross between Sleeping Beauty and Maleficent—I can't quite decide—leans in closer, her voice dripping with sarcasm. "You sound like a gold digger."

Without missing a beat, Cinderella throws her head back and laughs, "Well, maybe I am. And maybe tonight's my night!"

Hearing Cinderella's unabashed declaration and the laughter that follows sends a fresh wave of nerves coursing through me. It's one thing to be up for auction for a good cause; it's another entirely to navigate the murky waters of post-auction expectations.

"Does this mean there are going to be certain expectations with whatever guy ends up winning the bid for me?" I ask. The words feel heavy, loaded with implications I hadn't fully considered until now.

Stacy, quick to sense my growing unease, reassures me with a dismissive wave of her hand.

"Oh, please, Al, this is a classy affair. It's not that kind of date." But then, a mischievous glint appears in her eye, the kind that usually precedes her most outrageous ideas. "Well, unless you want it to be," she teases, a sly smile playing on her lips.

I can't help but laugh, shaking my head at her audacity. "Stace, you're terrible," I say, though the humor in my voice betrays my faux indignation. It's hard to stay worried with Stacy around; her ability to lighten the mood is a testament to our years of friendship.

Stacy just shrugs, unrepentant. "Hey, there are worse guys to be going out with tonight. You've seen the crowd—tons of rich, eligible bachelors out there."

Her gaze sweeps over the room as if to punctuate her point before settling back on me.

"And let's be real, you could stand to spend a night out with a nice, handsome man instead of yet another evening in the kitchen perfecting your béarnaise sauce."

Stacy knows me too well; my penchant for losing myself in the kitchen—especially when life outside it feels too chaotic—is no secret.

"You may have a point," I concede.

Peeking through the curtain, I can't help but let out a low whistle at the sea of glamorous attendees. It's like stepping into a scene from one of those movies where everyone is impossibly beautiful, sipping ridiculously expensive champagne.

They're the kind of people I've only ever observed from the safety of my kitchen, cooking them dishes that cost more than my rent.

"Honestly, what would I even say to a guy like that? 'So, how do you like your truffles? Shaved over gold leaf, or just straight out of the diamond-encrusted tin?'" I ask Stacy with sarcasm.

"Just smile and pretend you're having the time of your life," she advises, a grin tugging at the corners of her lips. "Besides, it's not like either of us would be able to afford a helicopter ride on our salaries. This might be your only shot to see New York from above without baking a cake for a billionaire's birthday party."

With a deep breath, I straighten up, adopting what I hope is a convincingly carefree smile. Stacy's right—this isn't just about the auction or a date; it's about stepping out of my comfort zone and trying something new. And if I get to soar over the city in a helicopter while doing it, who am I to complain?

But the part of me that's more comfortable wielding a spatula than engaging in small talk with the city's elite is seriously contemplating a tactical retreat. Just when the idea of bolting becomes dangerously appealing, however, it's my turn.

Stacy, sensing my last-second hesitation, locks eyes with me.

"You look insanely hot, Al," she assures me with the confidence of a general rallying her troops. "You've totally got this." Her words are the nudge I need, a reminder that I'm not just here to brave my social anxieties but to make a difference, however small it might seem.

Taking a deep, steadying breath, I channel every ounce of courage I possess and step out from behind the safety of the curtain. I plaster on my biggest, most dazzling smile—the one I reserve for successfully executing a flawless dinner service on a Saturday night.

Think of the kids, I silently repeat to myself, turning it into a mantra.

And that's when I see him.

CHAPTER 2

PATRICK

Every auction has its own surprises, but none quite like her—a vision in coveralls that challenged my every expectation and instantly commanded my full attention.

Here I am, nursing my second whiskey of the evening, each sip less satisfying than the last. The auction's buzzing energy seems to evaporate before it reaches me, leaving a dull hum in its wake.

To my right, a woman whose beauty would typically demand my full attention is making what could only be described as a valiant effort to engage me. Her name, something floral, escapes me as soon as she mentions it.

"So, Patrick, what brings a man like you to an event like this?" Her voice is smooth, a practiced melody of interest and allure.

"Charity," I answer, swirling the amber liquid in my glass. "And a temporary escape from the monotony of my own kitchen."

She laughs, a sound that's supposed to be charming. "A kitchen? I would've taken you for the Wall Street type. You have that air about you."

I offer a half-smile, the kind that usually suffices in these situations. "Executive chef, actually. My kitchen, my rules. Wall Street's a different kind of jungle."

"Ah, a man who can cook," she purrs, edging closer. "I find that incredibly sexy. Maybe you could show me your culinary skills sometime."

Under different circumstances, I might have entertained the thought. Tonight, however, the idea of extending this evening feels more like a chore. "Maybe," I say noncommittally, my attention already waning.

Just as I'm about to signal the bartender for another escape route—preferably something stronger—a stir at the edge of the stage captures my attention. The crowd's restless murmuring shifts, focusing on a new figure stepping into the limelight.

Petite, with curls of gold tumbling around her shoulders, she walks with an unexpected mix of confidence and confusion, as if she's as surprised by her presence on the stage as I am mesmerized by it.

Her outfit, an unlikely choice of coveralls with the sleeves tied around her waist and aviator sunglasses pushed up into her hair, somehow adds to her allure rather than detracting from it. It's audacious, it's different, and goddamn, it's sexy.

In an instant, my boredom evaporates, replaced by an intense curiosity and an undeniable pull. Who is she?

What's her story? And why does the sight of her feel like a jolt of electricity to my system?

Our eyes meet—a brief, electric exchange that brands her vivid green gaze into my memory. Up until this point, my plan for the evening was simple: contribute to a good cause, secure a neat tax deduction, and mentally archive the night as just another societal obligation fulfilled. Yet, there she stands, transforming my neatly laid plans into afterthoughts.

She arouses me from the moment I lay eyes on her. My cock pulses to life, and all I can think about is slipping her out of those coveralls, her body underneath no doubt perfect.

I have to have her.

"Ladies and gentlemen, let's turn our attention to the next exciting opportunity of the evening. We're thrilled to introduce a truly adventurous date with the lovely Allie. A chance to see New York City like never before, but I won't spoil the surprise just yet. Let's give a warm welcome to Allie!"

The auctioneer's voice fills the room, effortlessly weaving excitement and mystery into the introduction. He pauses, allowing the anticipation to build, a smile playing on his lips as he gestures toward the stage.

"Here she is, folks, in all her grace and charm. A bit shy under the bright lights, but don't let that fool you—there's an adventurous spirit waiting to share an unforgettable evening with one lucky bidder. Who's ready to take that leap and discover what New York has in store?

"Let's start the bidding at a modest one thousand dollars, shall we?" the auctioneer suggests, his voice echoing confidently through the ballroom. Hands shoot up almost immediately, signaling the crowd's eagerness. The bids climb quickly, the numbers jumping from one thousand to two thousand, then four thousand with enthusiastic shouts and competitive gestures.

"Five thousand to the gentleman in the back!" the auctioneer calls out, his eyes scanning the room for the next contender. The pace quickens, the figures climbing as the excitement builds. "Six thousand here! Do I hear seven?"

"Seven thousand!" comes a call from the side, a determined bidder not willing to back down.

The auctioneer nods, his gaze sweeping across the room. "Seven thousand dollars! Who will give me eight?"

A pause, then "Eight thousand" rings out clear and strong from another part of the room.

The auctioneer's grin widens. The bids now come in with a rhythm that speaks to the captivated interest Allie has garnered. "Eight thousand going once, twice ... anybody want to make it ten?"

There's a moment of suspense, a collective breath held, then broken by the assertive voice of a new bidder. "Ten thousand dollars."

The declaration silences the room for a split second, marking a significant leap in the stakes. The auctioneer, visibly pleased with the turn of events, beams as he addresses the crowd. "We're at ten thousand, folks! Can I hear eleven?"

An older gentleman, with a confident flick of his wrist, raises his paddle. "Eleven thousand here," he announces, voice steady and sure.

Not to be outdone, I lift my paddle, catching the auctioneer's eye. "Twelve thousand," I state, my voice carrying over the murmur of the crowd.

A younger guy, eager and perhaps a bit reckless, jumps in. "Thirteen!" he shouts, a blend of challenge and excitement in his tone.

The auctioneer's eyes gleam with the thrill of the chase. "Thirteen thousand, do I hear fourteen?" he calls out, his gaze flitting between us, the masters of this escalating duel.

"Fourteen thousand," the older man counters without hesitation, his paddle rising again.

I pause, letting the moment stretch, feeling the weight of the room's anticipation. Then, with a calm that belies my racing heart, I declare, "Fifteen thousand."

The auctioneer turns his attention to me, a nod of respect for the bid. "Fifteen thousand from the gentleman at the bar. Do we have sixteen?"

The young man, not ready to bow out, pushes further. "Sixteen!" he asserts, his determination painting him as a worthy adversary.

"Seventeen thousand," says the older man, his voice now carrying a hint of challenge.

With a glance toward Allie, who watches the proceedings with both awe and curiosity, I steel myself for the next leap.

"Eighteen thousand," I say, locking eyes with her for a fleeting moment.

The auctioneer, basking in the excitement of the bidding war, turns to the crowd. "Eighteen thousand going once ... going twice ..."

The tension is palpable, a thick cloak enveloping us all as we wait for the final hammer. In this scenario, amidst a sea of onlookers, the stakes are more than monetary—they're a pledge, a declaration of intent and interest, masked beneath the veneer of philanthropy.

"Twenty thousand!" calls out the younger man, a sneer appearing on his lips after he says the words as if he's convinced he's clinched the win.

The room is charged, every eye locked on the unfolding drama of the bidding war. The rapid climb of the bidding has become the evening's main spectacle, drawing curious glances from every corner of the ballroom. Even those backstage, previously absorbed in their own preparations, find themselves drawn to the edge of the curtains, craning their necks to witness the battle of wills and wallets.

Feeling the weight of the room's anticipation, I lean back in my chair, a sigh escaping me. This isn't my typical way of handling business at an auction—I prefer to keep my wealth under the radar, letting my culinary achievements speak for themselves. Yet here I am, caught in a game that's strayed far from its starting point.

It's time to end this.

I stand, my voice cutting through the crowd's whispers and murmurs. "Twenty-five thousand," I announce, loud and clear, the finality in my tone unmistakable.

A collective gasp sweeps through the ballroom, a wave of shock at the sudden jump. Heads turn, whispers grow louder, but my focus narrows down to one thing—the blonde on the stage.

Her reaction is immediate and unguarded. Eyes wide, mouth slightly agape, she's a picture of stunned beauty. With the spotlight casting her in an ethereal light, I'm captivated.

The auctioneer, momentarily taken aback as well, quickly regains his composure. "Twenty-five thousand! Any counters?" he challenges the room, though his tone suggests he knows the game is all but over.

The ballroom falls silent, and the previous contenders bow out with nods and murmured concessions, recognizing the conclusion of the bidding war. No paddles rise, and no voices dispute. It's an unequivocal victory, won not by the monetary amount but by the statement it makes.

As the auctioneer declares, "Sold, for twenty-five thousand dollars!" the applause is automatic, a ritual acknowledgment of the auction's highest bid.

For me, however, the ceremony fades into the background, overshadowed by the lady on the stage across the room. Her expression shifts from shock to a complex mix of emotions—gratitude, curiosity, perhaps even intrigue.

As the applause diminishes, the auctioneer makes his way over to me, his hand extended in gratitude. "Mr. Spellman, your generosity tonight is unparalleled. Thank you for your wonderful donation to the Bright Futures Foundation. Your contribution will make a significant difference."

I shake his hand, allowing myself a brief moment of satisfaction. Of course, supporting the charity was my initial intent. The Bright Futures Foundation's mission to provide opportunities for underprivileged children is a cause close to my heart, a reminder of the bigger picture beyond the glitz of tonight's event.

Yet, as much as I'm committed to the cause, I can't deny that my focus has shifted, honing in on a singular point of interest—Allie.

The excitement bubbling within me is a rare sensation that I haven't felt in quite some time. It's a heady cocktail of anticipation, curiosity, and, admittedly, a touch of nervousness. The auctioneer's instructions to head backstage to finalize the payment and meet my date for the evening only heighten my senses.

I make my way through the crowd, nods and murmurs of congratulations following me, my thoughts solely on the upcoming encounter.

I can't remember the last time I was this excited. The evening, which started as a routine gesture of philanthropy, has morphed into the beginning of something entirely unexpected.

As I make my way backstage, I'm intercepted by the older gentleman who was bidding against me. There's a warm smile on his face, a stark contrast to the competitive intensity from earlier.

"Patrick is it?" he starts, extending his hand. "I just wanted to thank you for making the auction quite the spectacle. Haven't had that much fun in a while."

I shake his hand, finding his demeanor surprisingly congenial. "Glad to hear it. It was quite the bidding war, wasn't it?"

He chuckles, nodding. "Indeed, it was. Allie looked like she'd be a fun gal to take out, but I'm glad it was you who won her over in the end. Make sure you show her a good time, will you?"

There's sincerity in his words, and I can't help but feel a sense of respect for the man. "I plan to. Thank you. It was all in good fun and for a great cause."

He pats my shoulder with a grandfatherly affection before parting ways, leaving me with a sense of warmth and an unexpected camaraderie.

My brief moment of reflection is interrupted as I catch the glare of the younger man who'd also been in the fray. His look is sharp, a silent challenge lingering in his eyes, but no words are exchanged. His demeanor doesn't faze me; instead, it reinforces the frivolous nature of his participation.

I nod in acknowledgment, though he offers no response. I turn away, leaving the silent standoff behind.

The backstage area is a hive of activity, but my mind is singularly focused. The previous encounters fade into the background, inconsequential in the grand scheme of things. My anticipation builds with every step, eagerness, and curiosity about the woman who's unwittingly turned an ordinary evening into an adventure I hadn't anticipated, guiding my movements.

CHAPTER 3

ALLIE

Backstage is a whirlwind of energy, but it's nothing compared to the storm raging inside me. I'm still reeling, unable to fully grasp that a bidding war—over me—just shattered the evening's records. Stacy, in all her mermaid glory, is practically vibrating with excitement next to me.

"Did you see that, Al? The record bid! That's you, girl! You're the queen of the auction!" Stacy's enthusiasm is infectious, her squeals of delight echoing off the walls.

I manage a laugh, though my mind is miles away, replaying the last few moments on stage. "I can't believe it either. Did that really just happen?"

"Yes, that just happened! And let's talk about Mr. High Roller," Stacy nudges me with a conspiratorial grin, her eyes sparkling with mischief. "I mean, hello, is he not the hottest thing on two legs? That bidding was intense!"

Ah, Mr. High Roller. Patrick. Even his name triggers a fresh wave of butterflies in my stomach. From the moment our eyes met, something shifted. It wasn't just his bid that caught my attention; it was him.

Tall, undeniably handsome, with a presence that seemed to pull the air from the room. His hair, a perfect balance of tousled and styled, gave him a carefree yet sophisticated vibe. And those eyes—intense, captivating—as if they could see right through me.

But it was more than just his physical appearance. It was the aura around him, all confidence and mystery. He stood there amidst the opulence and the glamour like a lighthouse in a stormy sea, a beacon of calm and assurance.

His physique spoke of strength and discipline. He was the kind of man you'd imagine in a smoky, dimly lit room, a glass of whiskey in hand, discussing art, life, and love with an intensity that would cause a woman to hang on his every word.

"I wasn't expecting him to be so ... hot," I confess, feeling a flush creep up my neck. The word feels inadequate to describe the jolt his presence sent through me, the way my heart seemed to skip a beat at the sound of his voice each time he outbid someone.

Stacy's laughter pulls me back to the moment. "Girl, you hit the jackpot! Not only did you break a record, but you also got yourself a date with the most eligible bachelor in the room. This is going to be epic!"

I can't help but smile, caught up in the excitement of what's happened. Yet, beneath the chaos and the banter, a thread of curiosity weaves its way through my thoughts. Who is Patrick, really? And what does this unexpected, thrilling connection mean for both of us?

"There's more to it, Stace," I finally admit, my voice dropping to a whisper. "I want him. Like, really want him."

Stacy blinks, her excitement dialing down a notch as she misreads my jittery confession. "Hey, Al, you know just because he put in the highest bid doesn't mean you owe him anything, right? This isn't some archaic barter system. You don't have to sleep with the guy."

Lost in thought, I can't help but imagine what it would be like to be with Patrick—not just a date, but to really be with him. It's a thought that sends a shiver down my spine, an unfamiliar blend of excitement and nervousness.

Stacy catches the far-off look in my eyes and the slightest hint of a blush on my cheeks. "Wait a minute," she says, a sly grin forming. "Allie, are you thinking about sleeping with him?"

I'm caught off guard, my thoughts exposed under the bright backstage lights. My nervous chuckle breaks free, an attempt to deflect. "What? No, I mean—"

"Oh, come on!" Stacy bursts out laughing, her amusement clear. "You totally are! I can see it all over your face. You're already fantasizing about it!"

My cheeks burn hotter, a silent confirmation of my unspoken desires. Stacy's laughter echoes around us, but my own racing heart drumming in my ears drowns out the sound. The very idea that I'm considering something so bold, so unlike me, with a man I don't know is both thrilling and terrifying.

"Stace, shush!" I hiss, glancing around to ensure no one else has caught on to our conversation. "It's not like that. I mean, I don't even know him."

"Uh-huh, sure," Stacy teases, one eyebrow raised in suspicion.

I can't help but laugh despite the embarrassment. Stacy has a way of making everything seem lighter and less daunting. "Okay, okay, you got me. But seriously, is there a rule about this? It feels like uncharted territory."

Stacy loops her arm through mine, her laughter subsiding into a warm smile. "Honey, the only rule is to follow your heart. And if your heart is currently fantasizing about a certain handsome bidder, then who am I to judge?"

Her words, meant to comfort, only stir the pot of confusion and curiosity simmering within me. Patrick has sparked something unexpected, a desire I can't quite quell. As Stacy guides me through the backstage chaos, I realize I'm standing on the edge of something entirely new, unsure but undeniably intrigued about where it might lead.

I sigh, the image of Patrick's intense gaze burning the back of my eyelids. "There's just something about him. It's not just his looks; it's the vibe he gives off. Confident, but not in an obnoxious way. It's like he knows what he wants and isn't afraid to go after it."

Stacy nods, her expression thoughtful. "Well, damn. That does sound enticing. But babe, don't forget, you're quite the catch yourself. This guy just dropped a small fortune to spend time with you. Clearly, he sees something special."

Just as Stacy is teasing me about the nonexistent dating auction ethics, he rounds the corner.

The sudden eye contact hits me like a live wire, sparking something wild and reckless inside me. At that moment, any thoughts about rules or what is considered proper vanish. I want this man. He's the epitome of walking, talking gorgeousness—smooth, undeniably sexy, with an aura that pulls me in like a magnet.

His voice, a low rumble that seems to resonate directly with my pulse, washes over me, turning my insides to mush.

"Hello, I'm Patrick," he says, his introduction directed at both of us, but his intense gaze locked on me. It's as if he sees me, really sees me, and I feel like the only woman in the world.

Stacy, ever the wing woman, picks up on the electricity crackling between us and makes a quick exit, her giggle trailing behind her like the perfect punctuation to this unexpected moment.

"Hi, I'm Allie," I manage to get out, my voice sounding oddly high-pitched to my own ears as we shake hands. No man has ever had this effect on me. For a second, I'm utterly speechless, a rare state for someone who usually has a quip for everything.

Patrick smiles a genuine, heart-stopping smile that makes me feel both incredible and slightly dazed. "Allie," he repeats, my name rolling off his tongue like music. "I've been looking forward to meeting you."

I blink, trying to regain some semblance of composure. "Well, here I am," I say, aiming for witty but landing somewhere closer to awkward. "And here you are, making history with your big bid tonight."

He chuckles, the sound warm and grounding. "I'd say we both made a bit of history, wouldn't you? And for a great cause, too."

"Absolutely," I agree, finding my footing again in the conversation. "Though I must admit, I never expected to be part of a bidding war. It's not exactly a typical Thursday for me."

"Nor for me," Patrick admits, his gaze still locked on mine with an intensity that's both thrilling and a tad overwhelming. "But I'm beginning to think it might just be one of my better Thursdays."

The way he says it sends a flutter through my heart. This incredibly handsome, impossibly charming man is standing here with me, and for the life of me, I can't think of anywhere else I'd rather be.

Stacy's earlier teasing about rules and expectations seems a world away now. All I know is that I'm caught up in a moment that feels like the start of something, an entirely new and exciting something.

Before I can even think of what to say next, we're interrupted by a woman who must have orchestrated this whole affair. She's all efficiency and grace, a whirlwind of thanks and congratulations.

"Patrick, I cannot thank you enough for your generosity tonight," she beams at him, but his eyes never waver from me, not even for a second. "Your contribution is the highest of the evening, and it will go a long way in supporting our cause."

She then turns to me, her smile just as warm. "And Allie, thank you for being part of this. Your participation has brought us this wonderful outcome. We hope to see you again next year."

She's off before I can muster a response, leaving behind a slip of paper with Patrick that I assume details our impending adventure.

The intensity of Patrick's gaze should have me squirming, but instead, it makes me feel like we're the only two people in the room. "So, would it be all right if I picked you up for our date tomorrow evening?" he asks with a slight tilt of his head. "Friday night seems like the perfect time for a bit of fun in the sky."

"That would be great," I find myself saying more eagerly than I intended. We swap numbers, a transaction that feels both mundane and charged with anticipation.

As if the night couldn't be any more like a scene out of a movie I'd swoon over, he lifts my hand and presses a kiss to the back of it. It's old-fashioned and ridiculously charming, and it sends a shockwave right through me.

I watch him walk away, every cell in my body acutely aware of the absence of his presence. It's like all my blood has decided to take a field trip to my lady zone, leaving me light-headed and more than a little enamored.

"Earth to Allie," Stacy's voice cuts through my stupor, a teasing lilt in her words. You look like you just saw a ghost—a very hot, very charming ghost."

I blink, trying to anchor myself back to reality. "I think I might just faint," I admit, half-joking but also half-serious.

"It's like all the blood in my entire body decided to focus on one particular area."

Stacy bursts into laughter, looping her arm through mine as we navigate our way out of the backstage area. "Well, if that's the effect he has on you with just a kiss on the hand, I can't wait to hear about the date."

I can't help but laugh along; the absurdity of the situation is not lost on me. "Yeah, if I survive it without combusting, it'll be a miracle."

As we make our way out, I can't shake the feeling that I'm on the cusp of something wildly unpredictable. Patrick, with his captivating gaze and gentle manners, has already turned my world upside down, and we haven't even been on our date yet.

"Stace, what if I'm not ready for this?" I whisper, a sudden surge of nervousness washing over me.

Stacy stops, turning to face me with a serious expression. "Allie, this is about having fun, about experiencing something new. There's no pressure for anything more. Just go, enjoy the helicopter ride, and who knows? Maybe it'll be the adventure of a lifetime."

Her words are a balm helping to soothe the hurricane of emotions inside me. "You're right," I say, taking a deep breath. "Adventure of a lifetime, here I come."

CHAPTER 4

PATRICK

I watch Allie take the stage once more, dressed in those same coveralls that first caught my eye. There's a difference this time, though—her gaze locks onto mine, loaded with a promise, a challenge, and it's the most intoxicating thing I've ever felt.

The bidding starts, a flurry of numbers flying around the room, but none of it registers. All I can focus on is the way she moves with a confidence that's as alluring as it is captivating. It's as if we're alone, caught in our own little world where the rules of etiquette don't apply.

I can't stand the suspense, the slow climb of numbers. With a decisive lift of my hand, I respond to an amount that silences the room—a bid that says more about my intent than any words could. The auctioneer catches the shift in the atmosphere, his eyes twinkling with understanding as he looks between us.

"She's all yours," he declares, his voice carrying a note of finality that seems to echo in the suddenly still ballroom.

I rise from my seat, the sound of my chair scraping against the floor echoing in the hushed space. As I make my way toward the stage, I realize everyone else in the ballroom is gone. The distance closes, step by step until I'm standing before her, the electric charge between us a living thing.

"Have you come to claim your prize?" Allie teases, her voice a sultry melody that pulls me in.

Without a word, I close the gap, my arm wrapping around her waist to draw her close. The world fades away as I lean in, capturing her lips in a kiss that seals the promise of what's to come—a kiss that's both a beginning and an answer to the unspoken questions swirling between us.

The kiss deepens, driven by a hunger that's been building since the moment we first locked eyes. It's passionate, demanding, a declaration made not in words but in touch, in taste, in the unyielding hold we have on each other. And when we finally break apart, the look in Allie's eyes tells me everything I need to know—this is just the start of our adventure.

We stand there on the stage, the world around us still blurred into insignificance. There's a sense of rightness, of inevitability, as if everything that's happened tonight has been leading up to this moment.

"Allie," I whisper again, my voice a low rumble filled with anticipation. "Ready for that date?"

Her response sends a thrill through me, "I'm ready for whatever you want to do with me—or to me." The playful challenge in her eyes is unmistakable as she begins to untie the sleeves of her coveralls and pull them down, a move that's both bold and incredibly sexy.

But just as the vanishing fabric starts to reveal more skin, a jarring sound cuts through the thick tension—a persistent, annoying alarm. It pulls me back, away from Allie, away from what was about to unfold.

I wake up with a start, the dream evaporating like mist under the morning sun. I'm in my home office, not the auction, and I try to shake the dream that felt all too real. The room is quiet, save for the alarm ringing from my phone. I stand as I turn off the alarm, stretching out the stiffness, the remnants of the dream still flashing in my mind.

Time to get focused. My date with Allie is today. A smile tugs at the corner of my lips, the excitement for what's to come igniting once again. That dream, as vivid and tempting as it was, is just a precursor to the possibilities that lie ahead. Allie, with her infectious laugh and those captivating green eyes, is waiting.

After selecting the perfect ensemble for the evening—a crisp, tailored shirt paired with dark jeans that strike a balance between casual and refined—I decide to check in on Caleb. My twenty-six-year-old law student son has carved out his own slice of independence in the spacious third story of my Brooklyn brownstone. With a set of stairs leading directly to his apartment, he enjoys a level of privacy most young men his age would envy.

As I ascend the stairs and enter his apartment, I find Caleb lounging on the sofa, absorbed in some TV show. He's inherited traits from both of his parents: my jawline and intense gaze. But he has his Latino mother's skin, along with her dark, expressive eyes.

It's an arresting combination, and there's no denying Caleb is a handsome guy. His sharp wit and intelligence only add to his appeal, making him not only good-looking but genuinely interesting to be around.

"Hey, Caleb," I greet, leaning against the doorway. "Got a minute?"

He glances over, a quick, assessing look that shifts into a warm smile. "Sure, Dad. What's up?"

"Just wanted to touch base before I head out. You got plans this weekend?" I ask, folding my arms across my chest.

Caleb mutes the TV, turning to face me fully. "Actually, yeah. Mike's getting married next month, remember? This weekend's the bachelor party. We're heading upstate."

"Ah, that's right," I nod, recalling the details. "Sounds like it'll be a good time. You'll be gone the whole weekend, then?"

"Yeah, leaving in a few hours and coming back Sunday night," he confirms, a hint of excitement in his voice. It's rare to see him so animated about social plans; Caleb's usually more reserved, a trait he definitely didn't inherit from me.

I chuckle, the ease between us a testament to the close relationship we've nurtured over the years. "Make sure to keep an eye on Mike. We don't want him doing anything too crazy before the big day."

Caleb laughs. The sound is rich and full. "Don't worry, Dad. I've got it under control. We're just looking to have some fun, nothing wild."

I study him for a moment, pride swelling in my chest. "I know you do. Just be safe, all right?"

He meets my gaze, his expression softening. "Always am. You don't need to worry about me. So, what about you, Dad?" Caleb suddenly turns the table, a hint of curiosity lighting up his eyes. "Got anything special planned for tonight?"

I hesitate for a moment, caught off guard. My love life, or the lack thereof, isn't typically on the agenda for our talks.

"Not much, just a quiet evening planned," I respond, deliberately vague. Sharing details about my date, especially one as unconventional as this one is, feels like crossing an invisible line I've drawn in the sand over the years.

Caleb's sharp enough to pick up on my evasion; however, a playful smirk appearing on his face. "Come on, I can tell you're lying. What's going on? Got a hot date or something?"

I can't help but chuckle at his persistence, appreciating his tact in not pushing too hard. "Let's just say I'm keeping my options open. It's nothing for you to worry about."

He raises his eyebrows, clearly amused, but nods in understanding. "All right, I won't pry. But I'm here if you want to tell me about it. Or, you know, need any advice," he says, the last part dripping with a teasing sarcasm that only a son can pull off.

"Thanks, Caleb. I'll keep that in mind," I reply, the warmth in my voice reflecting my appreciation for his offer, no matter how sarcastically it was stated. "Just make sure you have a good time this weekend. And call me if you need anything, okay?"

"Will do, Dad. And don't worry about me. Focus on having a fun night yourself," he says, his tone sincere. There's an understanding between us, a mutual respect that's always underpinned our relationship. Caleb knows when to step back, just as I know when to offer him the space he needs to grow and make his own decisions.

I snatch up my Audi R8 keys, the sleek machine a perfect match for my love of things that are cool without trying too hard. I start the car, the engine purring to life, a comforting backdrop to the anticipation bubbling inside me.

I pull up Allie's address on my phone and plug it into the GPS. My eyebrows knit together when I see it's in Brownsville. It's a far cry from the leafy streets of my own neighborhood of Park Slope. I can't help but feel a twinge of worry—she lives in a rough part of Brooklyn.

As I drive, I tell myself she's been doing fine without me worrying over her. But man, it's hard not to feel protective.

Pulling up to her building does nothing to ease that itch. It's clearly seen better days. My car sticks out like a sore thumb, and I can't shake off a sense of unease about Allie calling this place home.

As I park the Audi, I try to shove aside my worrisome thoughts. Allie's made it this far on her own, but damn if I don't want to show her a different side of life.

Stepping out, I'm hit with an unexpected resolve. This isn't just a date anymore—it's a chance to really get to know each other, to see beyond the surface. I become acutely aware that I want this night to turn into something more. Making my way to her door, I feel like I'm about to cross into a new chapter of my life.

I approach Allie's building, and the surroundings do little to lift my spirits. It's the kind of place where the trash seems to have its own ecosystem. The buildings are graffitied, and the windows grimy.

To my relief, her building's front door is locked. I buzz, announcing myself, and the door clicks open, granting me entry into a hallway that's seen better days. The carpet's threadbare, and the lights flicker. I navigate the narrow corridor, the numbers on the doors ticking down until I finally reach hers.

Knocking on the door, I try to brace myself, but nothing can prepare me for the moment she opens it. "Wow," slips out before I can stop it.

"We said casual, right?" she laughs, stepping back to let me in. Her version of casual is a knockout punch—denim jeans that fit just right and a simple white blouse that catches the light, making her look ethereal. Her makeup is minimal, and that smile of hers is like being handed a ticket to the best day ever.

"Uh, right," I manage to say, my usual charm taking a temporary leave. I step inside, glancing around the space. She catches my wandering gaze, a mischievous glint in her eye. "Don't tell me you're already regretting your winning bid?"

"On the contrary," I say, finding my footing again. "I'm starting to think I got the better end of the deal. And just for the record, I'm hoping our date lasts a bit longer than an hour in the air."

Her laughter fills the small space, setting me at ease. "Well, let's see how you feel after spending that hour with me, shall we?"

As she closes the door, the thought crosses my mind that this date, this moment, feels like the beginning of something unforgettable.

CHAPTER 5

ALLIE

Patrick looks every bit the model from a *GQ* photoshoot. From his perfectly tailored jeans that hug his frame in all the right places to that effortlessly styled hair, he's a vision from a magazine cover. His presence feels almost surreal against the backdrop of my modest apartment, like a misplaced piece from a glamorous jigsaw puzzle.

"Wow, did you get lost on your way to a photo shoot?" I tease.

Patrick chuckles, and the sound fills the room with a subtle warmth. "Ha! No, this is exactly where I want to be. Though I have to admit, I was half expecting a red carpet and a runway."

I can't help but laugh, the tension easing with our witty banter. "Sorry to disappoint, but the only red carpet you'll find here is probably from spilled wine from last week's dinner mishap."

He grins, and there's a genuine delight in his eyes that makes my heart do a little flip. "Then I'll consider myself duly warned."

I catch him taking in the less-than-stellar surroundings with a careful eye. There's no hint of disdain, more like concern that flickers across his face. It's endearing, really, seeing him try to mask it with a smile.

"Welcome to the glamorous side of Brooklyn," I say, a bit self-consciously.

Patrick's gaze softens. "As long as I'm with you, I'm sure it's the best tour I'll ever get."

With that, we head out. Stepping out onto the street, we make our way to his car—a sleek luxury ride that looks like it's been teleported from a futuristic utopia compared to the rest of the surroundings. He opens the door for me with a flourish that's both charming and slightly amusing, given our surroundings.

I notice Patrick's vigilant eyes scanning the area as we settle in. It's clear he's out of his element, but there's a protective vibe about him that I find unexpectedly reassuring.

"Always on guard, huh?" I comment as he slides into the driver's seat.

He offers a half-smile, his attention still partially on the street. "Let's just say I'm used to a different kind of jungle."

I can't help but find his concern sweet. "Well, don't worry. I've navigated this one for years. I'll keep you safe."

His laughter fills the car, easing the last traces of tension between us. "I'm counting on it."

As we pull away, the contrast between Patrick's world and mine couldn't be more stark. We merge onto the street, leaving my familiar neighborhood behind, and I find myself excited for the adventure ahead.

As Patrick navigates through the streets of Brooklyn, I lean back, allowing myself a moment to simply enjoy the ride. Being in a car in this part of the city feels like a novelty—I'm so used to being crammed into a subway car or chasing down a bus that the concept of personal transportation seems like a luxury. The smooth hum of the Audi's engine and the gentle caress of the leather seats are a welcome change.

Before long, we arrive at the helicopter tour spot in southern Brooklyn. My excitement bubbles over as we step out of the car. The idea of seeing the city from above as the sun sets, painting the skyline in hues of gold and orange, is thrilling.

The pilot greets us with a warm smile and launches into the safety briefing with a practiced ease. I hang on to every word, not because I'm particularly concerned about safety, but because I can't wait to get up in the air. The closer we get to takeoff, the more real it feels. This isn't just any date; it's an adventure.

As we approach the helicopter, Patrick places his hand on the small of my back, guiding me gently. The contact sends a shiver of excitement through me, a mix of anticipation for the flight and the electrifying touch of his hand. It's a small gesture, but it feels intimate, protective, and incredibly exhilarating all at once.

After climbing into the helicopter, I settle into my seat, buckling up as I steal a glance at Patrick. He seems completely at ease, a stark contrast to the flutter of nerves and excitement I'm feeling. But there's a look in his eyes, a shared excitement that tells me he's just as eager for this experience as I am.

As the engine roars to life and we lift off the ground, the city begins to shrink beneath us, transforming into a sprawling canvas of lights and shadows. The setting sun casts a golden glow over everything, making the view even more spectacular than I had imagined.

I see him watching me out of the corner of his eye, a smile playing on his lips. It's as if he's seeing the city anew through my eyes. As the helicopter soars higher, all of my anxiety seems to dissipate, leaving only the pure joy of the moment.

Patrick and I are squished together in the small space, and despite the fact that we've each got our own window to look out of, he's decided mine has the better view. Or maybe he just likes being this close. Either way, I'm not complaining. His body against mine is sending little zaps of electricity through me like I'm a human pinball machine.

When we land, my heart hasn't quite decided to slow down yet. It's doing this funny little dance, unsure if it's more jazzed about the insane views we just saw or the fact that Patrick's been in my personal bubble for the past hour. Trying to string together a coherent sentence feels like I'm learning to talk all over again as he guides me back to his car.

Once we're nestled inside the Audi, he throws me a curveball.

"Would you like to come to my place for dinner?" he asks, his voice smooth and confident.

Every rom-com and crime show I've ever seen is screaming in my head that going to a near-stranger's home isn't smart. But looking at him and thinking about the connection that's been buzzing between us all evening causes my yes to come out with barely a second thought. For good measure, though, I text Stacy the address because one can never be too careful.

Stacy's response is swift. She sends a selfie with an older couple in the background and a message that just says: *Have fun.*

Before I know it, we're pulling up to his brownstone in Park Slope, a neighborhood that's as charming as it is swanky. It fits Patrick like a glove—sophisticated, inviting, and unmistakably chic New York.

As he reaches over to open the car door for me, everything goes into slow-mo. I'm about to throw a casual thanks his way, but the look he's giving me zaps the word right out of my brain. It's like he's got electricity in his eyes, sparking something fierce within me. The air between us grows thick with this crackling tension like we're both aware something's about to happen, and neither of us wants to stop it.

He's close enough that I can catch the scent of his cologne, something rich and just a tad spicy. The vibe is intense, like the prelude to a thunderstorm, and I soak it all in, completely caught up in the anticipation.

Patrick closes that tiny gap between us, his hand finding a spot on my back that apparently has a direct line to my knees because they go all wobbly. It's a good thing I'm not standing. His touch is like a spark to dry tinder, setting off a warmth that spreads right through me.

We're all over each other in a heartbeat—kissing and touching in a way that's half desperate, half disbelieving of the insane amount of chemistry between us.

But right when things are heating up, Patrick pulls back with a grin. "You know, we're not teenagers anymore," he jokes, a hint of mischief in his voice. "Adults don't really make out in cars like this."

I let out a laugh, caught between frustration and amusement. "You sure about that? Because you're giving off some serious high school vibes right now."

He chuckles, and there's a warmth in his eyes that makes my heart do a funny little skip. "My apologies, madam. Allow me to retain some semblance of adulthood here."

I reach for the door handle, ready to step out and attempt to regain a bit of my composure. But before I can, Patrick's gentle reminder stops me. "Wait. Let me get that for you the proper way," he says, and there's something in the way he says it, a kind of old-school chivalry that's both charming and totally at odds with how we were just mauling each other.

So, I wait, watching as he strides around the front of the car, his gaze locked onto mine. It's a look full of hunger and promise, and it sends my pulse racing all over again. The air between us is electric with anticipation, and as he opens my door, his smile tells me everything I need to know.

Stepping out of the car, I'm practically vibrating with excitement, my thoughts a whirlwind of what-ifs and can't-waits.

Patrick's hand finds mine, his touch grounding yet thrilling, and as we head toward the door leading into his house, I can't help but think that whatever Patrick has planned, I'm more than ready for it.

"Lead the way," I say, my voice steady despite my racing heart.

CHAPTER 6

ALLIE

The moment Patrick opens the door to his place, it's like stepping into one of those daydreams I've had a million times—a Brooklyn brownstone straight out of a fairy tale, with its elegant charm and whispered tales of a life I've always wanted but never quite believed I could have. The place is stunning, with warm lighting that casts a soft glow over everything, making it feel like we've stepped into our own private world.

Who is this guy?

The question flickers through my mind as I take in the high ceilings and the intriguing art that adorns the walls. But the question dissolves as quickly as it appears because, in the next moment, Patrick's pulling me into him, and his lips find mine in a kiss that causes all rational thought to flee.

Patrick is a revelation. His body against mine feels solid and reassuring, the kind of presence that says without words that I'm safe in his arms. His taste is intoxicating, making me want to dive deeper and deeper.

His hands are everywhere, strong and gentle all at once. They map a path across my back and pull me closer until there's no space left between us. The kiss deepens and grows more urgent, as if we're both trying to communicate what we're feeling without breaking away to speak.

It's a rush of emotion and sensation that leaves me dizzy, my heart pounding in a way that says this is something special.

As we finally come up for air, I find myself caught in his gaze, and there's a vulnerability there that matches my own. Wrapped up in Patrick's arms in the middle of his beautiful home, everything else fades away. The questions, the doubts, the wondering about who he is—they all seem trivial compared to the connection between us.

This intensity is overwhelming and a little bit scary, but as I look up at him, I realize I wouldn't want to be anywhere else.

Catching our breath, the air between Patrick and me sparkles with an unspoken need. "You lead the way, or I might get lost in this mansion," I tease, trying to sound nonchalant despite being utterly captivated by the sophistication surrounding us.

Patrick's grin in response is all kinds of dangerous. "Getting lost could be the most exciting part of your night," he shoots back, his voice laced with promise.

"Oh, is that so?" I quip, matching his playful tone while my mind races ahead to what the night might hold. "And here I thought the evening couldn't get any more thrilling."

As Patrick begins to lead me up the stairs, I catch a glimpse of his kitchen through an open door, and it stops me mid-step. It's large and stunning—like something straight out of a high-end restaurant. Gleaming stainless steel appliances, an industrial-sized fridge, sprawling counters that never end, and an island that could easily seat a dozen.

It seems almost excessive, even for a rich executive chef. The sight leaves me momentarily awestruck, and my curiosity is piqued about the man leading me upstairs.

As we begin our slow advance toward his room, it's clear neither of us is in a hurry. Each step is punctuated by lingering touches and smoldering glances. Our clothes start to trail behind us, an urgency building with every moment we're together.

Reaching the landing, Patrick turns to me under the soft lighting, and the sight nearly steals my breath away. The play of shadows across his chest and arms highlights every muscle, every curve, and my fingers itch to explore.

Noticing my gaze, he raises an eyebrow, a mix of amusement and challenge in his eyes. "Like what you see?" he asks, his voice a low rumble that reverberates straight to my core.

"Absolutely," I admit without a shred of embarrassment, letting my eyes roam appreciatively. "The architecture in here is simply stunning."

Patrick laughs. It's a sound that wraps around me, warm and inviting. "Glad you approve," he says, pulling me close once again. "But just wait until you see the bedroom."

His skin feels smooth and inviting under my fingertips, and I can't resist the urge to let my hands roam a bit, marveling at what I find. He's solid and real and radiates a warmth that envelops me and draws me in.

"See something else you like?" Patrick's voice is a low rumble.

I look up at him through my lashes and give him a sexy smirk. "Just admiring the view," I reply, trying to sound playful yet sincere. "A helicopter ride over the city's got nothing on this."

He chuckles, takes my hand, and leads me into the bedroom, which is gorgeous and has a spectacular view of the downtown skyline.

"Come here."

I step toward him, and we begin to kiss, slow and sexy at first, then with more fire. He lifts my shirt, softly caressing my skin before raising it up and over my head and tossing it on the floor. I reach for his buttons, eagerly undoing each one before pushing his shirt off his shoulders, allowing it to fall behind him. I take a moment away from the kiss to run my hands over his strong, chiseled chest.

He pulls at my jeans before taking off his belt, hinting for me to take them off. Our mouths return to one another's, searching and seeking, devouring. He places his hands on my hips and pulls me against him. We're both in nothing but our underwear, Patrick's hardness straining the fabric of his boxer briefs. I can't believe how quickly I'm moving with him and how much I want him.

He kisses me long and deep, his cock pressed against my stomach, moans pouring from my lips as I savor the sensation of his body against mine. Without thinking, I reach down under his waistband and take hold of his hardness.

He's long and thick and feels perfect in my grasp. I stroke him slowly, a growl sounding from the base of his throat as I tease him. His hands reach around, settling on my ass, squeezing it firmly.

I stroke him faster, wanting to hear more of those sexy growls, and part of me wants him to erupt in my hand, all over my belly. But when his thumbs slip underneath the waistband of my panties and begin inching them down, I know he's got other things on his mind.

My panties fall to my ankles, and he's right there with a command.

"Bed. Now."

His tone doesn't leave any room for discussion. A shiver runs up my spine at the firmness of the direction.

I kind of love it.

I step backward, reach the bed, and sit down on it. My eyes drift to his massive erection, my pussy soaking wet from his touch and his kiss.

"Take off your bra."

Another irresistible command. I reach around, undoing the clasp, sliding the straps down my shoulders. He drinks in the sight of my bare breasts, and when I toss the bra aside, I realize that this is the first time I've been naked in front of a guy in a really long time.

He steps over to me, his erection just a few inches from my face. I can't wait any longer. I pull down his boxer briefs, his cock springing out in front of me. His manhood is freaking gorgeous. I can't resist leaning in, covering his length in kisses.

I'm rewarded for my efforts with sexy groans and growls. I want to do more, I want to take his cock into my mouth, but before I can, he swoops on top of me, laying me back onto the bed and placing his hand between my thighs.

"Oh... Oh my God..."

He spreads me open and finds my clit right away, rubbing me, teasing me, making slow, little circles that bring me close to orgasm so quickly that I can hardly breathe. His lips find my jaw, and he's kissing and touching me at the same time, the orgasm building.

"You look so fucking hot when you're about to come," he says, pure heat in his voice.

I can't even think of a response; the pleasure is so intense. I buck my hips into his hand, making damn sure he stays in the same place, making the same motions, luring me into a perfect trance. My body clenches, and my pussy contracts before pleasure erupts inside me.

He continues to touch me through the climax, and I open my eyes slightly. Patrick's still on top, gazing down at me with a sensual intensity as if he's in the middle of painting a masterpiece and wants to make sure every stroke is perfect.

My hands fall to my sides, my arms going limp, my chest rising and falling.

"You look spent already," he says with a grin. "But I'm not quite done with you."

He reaches down and grabs his cock, pushing it against my drenched pussy, teasing me, making me wait. The fucker knows just how much I want him, and he's loving every damn second of it.

"Please," I moan, placing my hands on his sculpted behind. "Please, Patrick."

"Protection," he mutters.

"On the pill. Just please, don't make me wait."

I press down on his rear, hoping to simply push him inside. But he holds still, the whisper of a grin forming on his lips as he takes more enjoyment out of teasing me.

Finally, mercifully, he thrusts forward. I'm soaked, and he glides into me with no effort at all. I wrap my legs around him, my walls stretching as he bottoms out deep inside me.

His first few thrusts are slow and deep, allowing me to get used to his size and thickness.

But he's soon going faster, harder, splitting me in half again and again until I can't feel anything but his huge cock pushing into me, his arm wrapped around my upper body, his muscles so hard and hot against me.

"Yes, *yes!*" I scream, the pleasure so intense that I can hardly think straight.

He moves his hand along the curve of my spine as he bucks into me, making damn sure I feel every inch of him stretching me, filling me. His right hand weaves into my hair, bringing my face against his for another deep kiss, the slapping sound of his body against mine filling the air.

I'm screaming, my throat hoarse, the delight so intense.

"Come for me, Allie," he growls. "Right now."

There's no resisting him even if I wanted to, and I most certainly do not want to. I shudder hard, and another orgasm, this one way more powerful than the first, rips through my body. He's right there with me, grabbing my hips and pulling me hard into him as he releases deep inside, filling my pussy to the brim.

As our climaxes fade, he falls to my side, lying on the bed beside me.

I don't know what to think. Never in my life have I even come close to experiencing what I just experienced with Patrick. Two crashing, exploding orgasms that he managed to coax out of me with little effort. Who the hell is this man?

He wraps his arm around me, pulling me close for another kiss.

"Hell of a date, gorgeous," he says.

"You're right about that."

I close my eyes and prepare to let sleep overtake me.

CHAPTER 7

PATRICK

I'm lying in bed with her head on my shoulder, and I'm in a state of total disbelief. She's asleep, her breaths even and peaceful against my chest, and the warmth of her body curled up next to mine. It gives me a feeling of comfort I didn't know I was missing.

It's strange, this contentment that's settled over me. I've always maintained a certain distance in my relationships, preferring fleeting connections over anything that hinted at permanence. But with Allie, it's different. There's something about her that whispers of possibilities, of unknown depths waiting to be explored.

As I watch her in the dim light, I gently brush a strand of hair from her face, and I can't help but let my mind wander to the less conventional aspects of my desires. The thought of introducing her to the other facets of my intimacy, the ones that require trust and a mutual understanding of boundaries. Would she be open to exploring with me, to pushing the limits of pleasure in a way that's new to her?

I imagine the contrast of leather against her soft skin and the intense exchange of power and control that makes bondage play so thrilling. Just the thought of it sends a rush of anticipation through me that makes me hot, mingling with a tenderness I hadn't expected to feel.

I've only shared this dangerous side of me with a few, and always with clear limits and mutual respect, Yet the idea of exploring it with her feels somehow different and more significant.

But it's not just about the physicality of bondage. It's the trust, communication, and vulnerability that comes with it —elements I find myself wanting to offer her. The lingering question, however, is whether she'd be willing to walk that path with me.

But for now, though, I push those thoughts aside, choosing instead to focus on the quiet intimacy of the moment. The way she fits against me feels right, like a puzzle piece clicking into place. And as I let myself drift to sleep, lulled by the rhythm of her breathing, I make a silent promise to tread carefully and not scare her away.

Tonight, it's enough just to have her here, to feel the gentle press of her body against mine, and to know that, for the first time in a long while, I'm not alone.

○○○

My cock's hard as stone when I wake up, the scent of Allie lingering all around me. I'm ready for round two, ready to claim her again, to make her mine. Except, when I reach out for her, I find nothing but cold sheets.

I bolt upright, a mix of confusion and annoyance setting in. I check the bathroom; no sign of her. Slipping on some pants, I search the house, but she's nowhere to be found. The house is silent, every room echoing back nothing but my own footsteps.

The quiet seems deafening compared to the warmth and laughter we shared just hours before. Did I screw something up? Or did she just bail without a word?

I'm not one to overthink things, get caught up in feelings, or jump to conclusions, but this vanishing act has caught me off guard. I'm baffled as to why she would just leave without so much as a note or a text.

Then I think that maybe I overlooked something in the bedroom so I go back and look again. But I find nothing. It's like she's disappeared into thin air.

This isn't how I expected the morning to go. An amazing night has twisted into a bit of a head-scratcher. For the first time in who knows how long, I'm rattled by someone's absence. I thought we had something worth exploring. I thought we really connected but now I'm not so sure. Maybe what I felt wasn't mutual, even if every instinct told me otherwise.

I let out a heavy sigh, feeling both frustrated and—strangely —disappointed. She seemed different from other women, deeper. But I have my pride. I'm not about to chase after someone who took off without a word. The idea leaves a sour taste in my mouth, and I decide to eat breakfast to try to counter it.

I finish buttoning up my shirt with a finality that matches my mood. I'm not one to dwell or run after someone who has clearly made their choice, even if, for a hot minute, I thought we had something worth exploring.

As I stand there, the sense of feeling cheated washing over me, I decide to focus on something grounding. Making breakfast seems like the perfect distraction, a way to move past the confusion of the morning. As I'm cracking eggs into a skillet, I hear the door opening, and for a split second, I feel hopeful that she's come back. But it's my son Caleb who comes walking in looking like he's been through the wringer.

My hopes are dashed; I greet him. "Hi, son. Rough night?"

"Morning, Dad," Caleb mumbles, his voice rough around the edges. He heads straight for the fridge, pulls out a bottle of water, and downs it with a thirst that speaks volumes about how his night went.

"Weren't you supposed to be gone all weekend?" I ask, turning back to the stove. The sizzle of the eggs fills the brief silence that follows.

Caleb leans against the counter, taking another long gulp before responding. "Yeah, it was wild. Mike had a bit of a meltdown. Got all guilty about cutting loose and ended up a drunken mess. We came back early this morning."

I chuckle, shaking my head. "Weddings bring out the best—and the worst—in people."

"Yeah, you can say that again." Caleb cracks a crooked smile, the first real sign of life I've seen in him since he walked in. "So, what about you? What did you get up to last night?"

I keep my eyes on the eggs and don't answer right away. The question hangs in the air, heavier than the smell of breakfast cooking. I flip the eggs, buying myself a moment to think. "Nothing much," I reply, keeping my tone nonchalant. The memory of Allie, of our night together, feels too personal to share, even with Caleb.

He studies me for a moment, clearly not buying it, but decides not to push. "All right, keep your secrets, old man," he teases, moving to grab a plate.

As we settle down to eat, the conversation shifts to safer topics—Caleb's upcoming finals, the latest news in the culinary world, anything but being left in the lurch by a woman in my own house.

I'll forget her in no time, I think, even as part of me knows it isn't true.

CHAPTER 8

ALLIE

Hopping on the train that morning, my head swirling with thoughts of last night. The memories have me grinning like an idiot at my reflection in the window. But then, the grin fades a bit as I wonder—*did I bail too soon?*

It's classic me: making decisions on the fly and worrying about them after the fact. It's not like I can do much about it now.

Stepping off the train onto my block, everything looks more worn out than usual. I feel like Cinderella the day after the ball. Patrick's place feels like a world away from the graffiti-tagged bricks and the smell of last night's takeout in the air.

I make my way to my apartment, and the second I open the door and step in, I see Stacy at the kitchen table. Her eyes light up like I just walked in carrying a birthday with candles.

She practically vaults from her seat, quivering with anticipation. "So? Spill! I want details, Al. I've been dying here!"

I hang up my bag by the door, debating how much to tell her. "Well, for starters, his place is straight out of a magazine, a brownstone in Park Slope."

Stacy's mouth is open, and she's hanging on every word. I can't help but laugh at her expression. "Go on ..." she says.

"And Patrick is ... something else. He's like if Mr. Darcy and James Bond had a love child. I had an incredible time."

"But then, why are you home so early?"

I flop down in the chair across from her, shrugging. "I don't know. I just felt like the night had reached its natural end."

Stacy looks at me like I have two heads. "So, wait, he didn't ask you to go? You just left?"

I wince. "When you put it like that, it sounds ... bad."

She rolls her eyes. "Only you, Al. Only you could have a fairy-tale night and turn it into a difficulty."

I lean back and think about last night. Despite the teasing, a part of me can't shake the feeling that maybe she's right.

"So, how steamy did it get?" she asks, clearly dying to hear the salacious details.

But I'm not biting. Some things feel too personal, too intimate to share, even with my bestie. "Let's just say it was memorable," I answer, sounding purposely vague.

"You're no fun," Stacy huffs. But then, seeing she's not going to get the dirt she's craving, she changes tactics. "Fine, be that way. But what about that selfie I sent you? Bet you're dying to know who the mysterious couple in the background was."

I nod, eager to shift the focus away from my own tale. "Yeah, who were they? Your babysitters for the night?"

Stacy bursts into laughter. "Something like that. That was the guy who bid on you, believe it or not. He and his wife ended up taking me to the aquarium. They're like the sweetest grandparents ever. They just wanted to contribute to the cause."

I can't help but smile at the thought—my wild night compared to her evening with doting grandparents at the aquarium. "That sounds adorable, actually."

"Yeah, it was." Stacy's grin fades slightly as she leans forward, her tone turning protective. "But back to you and Patrick. I need to know more."

I shake my head, not willing to share more. "He was a perfect gentleman. And, for the record, it was the best sex I've ever had." I feel a blush creeping up my cheeks at the admission, but it's the truth.

Stacy raises an eyebrow. "And yet, you left?"

"There was something about him," I say, struggling to articulate the mix of emotions I was feeling. "Something that made me nervous."

Stacy's expression softens, her usual bravado giving way to genuine concern. "If that was your gut feeling, then you did the right thing, no matter how good the sex was."

I nod, knowing she's right. My instincts have always guided me, and something about Patrick, as incredible as our night was, raised a red flag.

That's when Emily and Maya, our other two roommates, come into the kitchen, and I take it as an excuse to go to my room.

"I'm going to crack you open like a safe!" Stacy shouts after me, and I can't help but laugh as I shut my bedroom door.

Once I'm in my room, guilt begins to nibble at me. I kind of left Stacy thinking Patrick spooked me, which is not the case. It's more like he sent my heart into overdrive in the best possible way. But laying all that bare felt way too intense for breakfast conversation.

Growing up in foster care and not having a real family has left its mark. Stacy came into my life and has become the sister I never had. The truth is, I bolted from Patrick out of the sheer terror of getting my heart karate-chopped into pieces. Patrick, with his come hither eyes and magic hands, felt like a hurricane that could sweep me away. So, I hightailed it out of there.

After a bit of pondering in my room, I decide a shower might do me some good. But the second the water hits me, so does the memory of Patrick. And just like that, I'm back in his arms, the world outside a blur.

I can't help the grin that spreads across my face, thinking about how effortlessly he carried me through the evening, how every moment felt charged with electricity, even before anything sexual happened. It's funny how the mind wanders, especially when you're trying not to think about someone. I'm supposed to be scrubbing off the remnants of last night, yet all I can do is replay every laugh, every touch, and every look he gave me.

CHAPTER 9

ALLIE

In the back of the house at Verde Oliva, where I've been working as a sous chef for the last two years, I'm queen of the kitchen. I'm tasked with the noble duty of prepping the ingredients for our chef's special: gnocchi with a truffle parmesan sauce.

When I'm cooking, I'm like a conductor of an orchestra, where every ingredient hits its cue perfectly. The kitchen's buzzing, pans are clattering, and I am in my element, humming a tune that's stuck in my head. Lost in my chopping and dicing, my mind effortlessly slips back to Patrick, and I cut myself for the first time in years.

It's a minor cut on my finger, but it's enough to snap me back to reality as I run my finger under cold tap water. It's moments like these that remind me of the delicate balance between passion and precision, both in the kitchen and, apparently, in matters of the heart. I put on a Band-Aid and a glove before I finish prepping for the dinner special, my mind continuing to flash back to Patrick.

Chef Marco comes around the corner and looks at me. "Did you cut yourself, Allie?"

I sheepishly nod. "I did, Chef. The knife slipped, but I'm all good."

He gives me a condescending look and walks away.

Great, now I feel like an idiot.

Back at my station, I dive into finishing the gnocchi, temporarily suspending all thoughts of charming men. I focus on the task at hand, each movement precise and practiced. Proudly, I hand the plate over to Chef Marco, my confidence buoyed by the dish's undeniable excellence.

Marco sighs, picks up his fork and takes a bite. I watch him closely, not missing the brief flicker of surprise that lights up his eyes.

Gotcha.

However, it takes him no more than a heartbeat for his face to settle back into its usual stern mask. "It's lacking," he declares, setting the fork down with a finality that suggests the matter is closed.

"Lacking?" I can't hide the incredulity in my voice. "I'm sorry, Chef, but did we taste the same gnocchi? I think it's good, very good."

Marco fixes me with a withering look, but I stand my ground. "The sauce is too heavy, the gnocchi too soft," he says disdainfully.

"Too heavy?" I counter, my frustration growing. "The balance is perfect. And the gnocchi is exactly as it should be —light, pillowy—precisely the texture it should be."

"Try again," Marco says dismissively, waving me off, but I know I saw that initial spark of delight in his eyes.

Fuming, I stomp away. I saw that initial look on his face. He knew it was good. No, not just good—great.

But the more I think about it, the more I realize Marco has been edgy around me lately. It's like he's looking over his shoulder, watching his back in his own kitchen. And suddenly, it dawns on me—he's worried about being upstaged in his own restaurant—by me.

I taste the gnocchi again, and it is indeed excellent. It's crystal clear to me now—he's not just critiquing my cooking; he's trying to keep me in my place. But I also know I'm too much of an asset to him for him to even think about letting me go.

As I'm about to throw the gnocchi into the trash, I notice movement at the food prep window. It's Caleb, my ex-boyfriend. What the heck is he doing here? He waves at me like he's just dropped by for a casual visit.

I wipe my hands on my apron and walk over to see what he wants. Luckily, the restaurant hasn't opened yet, so I have time to chat.

He leans against the counter with a confident ease.

"Hey, Caleb," I say as I step out of the kitchen. "What brings you here?"

He smiles familiarly. "I was in the neighborhood and thought I'd say hi. Plus, I wanted to see the queen at work," he adds, gesturing back toward the kitchen.

"Really? That's it?" I ask with a smile. "You just wanted to pop by and say hello?"

"Well, not exactly. I'm interning with a lawyer who asked me where to find the best Italian food in the city, and obviously, I thought of this place—and you," he says.

I smile, remembering how sweet Caleb is. He's a great guy, and I'm not sure why I ended things, except that I just didn't think the relationship was going anywhere.

"So, you still happy working here?" he asks as if he's genuinely curious.

I hesitate before admitting, "Sure, but it's stressful, to say the least."

He leans in, lowering his voice to a conspiratorial whisper, "Is Chef Marco still being a complete dick?"

"Yes!" I say and burst out laughing.

"The reason I ask is that my dad is the owner and executive chef at Savor," he says, a note of pride in his voice.

Savor is the culinary Olympus of Williamsburg, Brooklyn. It's got a five-star rating and a mile-long waiting list. Although it's only been open for a few months, it's already getting rave reviews.

"He is? That's incredible, Caleb. I've heard it's amazing," I manage to say, trying to sound nonchalant and failing.

"Yeah, it's a great place. And, well, here's the thing," he continues, his tone serious, "he's looking for a new sous chef."

I feel my face get hot. "Seriously?"

He nods, smiling. "Seriously. I thought of you immediately. If you're interested, I could meet you there tomorrow morning, show you around, and introduce you to my dad."

"That would be fantastic!" I say immediately.

Caleb laughs, the sound rich and warm. "I figured you'd say that. So, you'll meet me there?"

"Of course," I say, more firmly this time, "It's a once-in-a-lifetime opportunity."

We set a time to meet, say our goodbyes and I float back into the kitchen. Finally, I think the universe is smiling at me. It makes Marco's attitude and the stress of his kitchen seem to fade away.

CHAPTER 10

PATRICK

I'm in the middle of dinner prep at the restaurant when Caleb pitches me on his ex's culinary skills.

"Mixing work and personal life, Caleb? You know how that can go." My voice is even but firm.

"Dad, she's phenomenal in the kitchen. Remember the handmade ravioli I brought over that one time? The one that had you staring off into space while you ate? That was hers."

I pause, recalling the dish. "It *was* impressive," I admit, my curiosity piqued despite my reservations. "What about her experience?"

"She's sous chef at Verde Oliva right now. She does their specials."

I know and like Verde Oliva. It's known for turning out high-quality dishes.

"Wait," I say. "Verde Oliva. That's Marco DiCampi's place, isn't it? She works for him? He's supposedly a grade-A asshole."

"Yup," Caleb says, "one and the same."

I'm impressed. "Well, if she's thrived under his reign for two years ..."

"Exactly my point, Dad," Caleb says.

"That's something," I admit grudgingly. Surviving in Marco's kitchen speaks volumes about her resilience and skill.

Changing gears, Caleb looks around the bustling kitchen. "Any chance I can grab something to eat while I'm here? The smell's killing me."

I shoot him a look, half amused, half exasperated. "Your appetite's going to bankrupt me one of these days," I joke, but I'm already reaching for ingredients. Caleb's my favorite person to cook for and always has been.

Within minutes, I've got scallops sizzling in a pan.

As I plate the dish, arranging the scallops with a drizzle of sauce, Caleb's eyes widen. "That looks incredible, Dad."

I carry the plate into my office, where we can continue our conversation away from the cooks in the kitchen. As Caleb dives in with gusto, I can't help but feel a twinge of pride. Cooking is my language, my way of connecting.

Between bites, he says, "You know, she's really passionate about cooking. It's not just a job for her; it's like her calling or something."

I nod, understanding that feeling all too well. "Passion's what separates the good from the great," I agree, suddenly intrigued by the idea of meeting someone with that level of dedication.

"Why the sudden need for a new sous chef anyway?" Caleb asks.

I sigh, leaning back in my chair. "Sarah is leaving. Her first baby is due at the end of the month, and she wants to be a stay-at-home mom. It's a big loss for the team, so I need someone to fill her shoes and get up to speed."

Caleb's eyes light up. "That's perfect timing, then. Your kitchen, her talent—it could be the perfect match."

I pause, considering the possibility of what he's saying. "Tell her to come by and drop off her resume," I say, already mapping out in my mind how I'd onboard a new sous chef with such little lead time.

Caleb's grin widens. "Already did that. I stopped there on my way over here."

I can't help but laugh, shaking my head at his forwardness. "Confident about your sales pitch, huh? Well, if she impresses me, we'll give her a trial run. See if she can handle the pressure of my kitchen."

Caleb nods in agreement. "Oh, she can."

Curiosity gets the better of me, and I ask, "Why do you care so much about what an ex is up to?"

He leans back, his plate clean, and looks me straight in the eye. "Because she's got real talent, Dad. And talent like that shouldn't be wasted. She deserves to be doing great things with it. We didn't work out, but the breakup wasn't bad, and she's a great person."

Hearing the conviction in Caleb's voice, I can't argue with that. Talent is the lifeblood of any great kitchen, and if she's as good as he claims, then maybe she's exactly what Savor needs right now.

Caleb wipes his mouth on a napkin and stands. "I should get going. I need to change before tonight. I have that client dinner for my internship," he says.

As he's about to leave, I can't resist a little jab, nodding toward the empty plate on the table. "Don't forget to wash that up at the dish area on the way out," I tell him, half-serious.

He laughs, the sound echoing in the office. "Ah, that'll bring back memories of my dishwasher days back in undergrad," he says, picking up the plate. It's a small reminder of how far he's come, from washing dishes in my kitchen to navigating the legal world by interning at a law firm.

With a final wave, Caleb heads out, leaving me alone with my thoughts. The conversation about the potential new hire lingers in my mind. Marco DiCampi, for all his faults, is undeniably talented, and his kitchen is a great proving ground. If she's managed to thrive there, she's got the kind of mettle I respect.

Once Caleb's gone, I step back into the fray of the kitchen, making sure everything's running smoothly.

Eventually, I retreat to my office, where I await the least favorite part of my day: the administrative side of owning a restaurant. It isn't glamorous, but it's necessary. As I sift through invoices and schedules, the thought of bringing in someone new, someone who's managed to hold her own in Marco's kitchen, keeps circling back into my thoughts.

I make a mental note to review her resume as soon as it comes in. If she's as good as Caleb says, I want to see it for myself.

As I plow through the paperwork, the restaurant's rhythm beginning to hum with the pre-dinner rush energy, my focus is abruptly redirected. The phone buzzes, and it's Alex, my front-of-house manager.

"Chef, there's a gentleman here asking to speak with you privately in your office," Alex's voice carries a note of curiosity, maybe even a hint of concern.

"Is there a reason you're bothering me with this instead of handling him yourself?"

"Normally, I would. But this guy ... he's a VIP. You're going to want to talk to him personally."

"Lead him back," I reply, my interest piqued. Who would request a private meeting now, of all times?

The man who steps into my office a few moments later is immediately familiar. He's in his sixties, well-dressed with understated elegance. There's a poised assurance about him and also a hint of menace, not overt but unmistakably there. His hair is jet-black, tinged silver on the sides, slicked back with care.

Luca Amato. Not only does he have a particular reputation around town, but he's dined at my restaurant more than a few times.

"Mr. Amato, to what do I owe the pleasure?" I ask as I stand to greet him.

"Luca, please," he insists, with a polite nod. "And as to why I'm here, let me begin by saying I've been a patron of your establishment since the doors first opened. You run a fine restaurant, Patrick."

I'm well aware of Luca's other reputation—that of a high-ranking member of the Italian mafia in New York.

"I'm honored to have your continued support, Luca."

My mind is already racing through potential scenarios—an extortion attempt seems the most likely reason for this visit, but then I catch myself—Luca Amato isn't the type to personally handle such matters. He has people for that.

Luca's next question catches me entirely off guard. "How much would it cost to rent out your entire restaurant for an evening, one night per month? Say, on a Tuesday? I'm thinking a full five-course meal, including wine and spirits."

I blink, processing the request. Renting out the entire restaurant is a big ask. "I'd need to crunch some numbers," I admit. "Calculate what we typically bring in on a Tuesday, figure out staffing, a menu, a wine list. It's a sizable undertaking."

"I understand."

"Why the whole place? Why not just a private room?" I probe, curious about his intentions.

Luca chuckles, an amusing sound. "Do you have a private room I've somehow missed all these years?"

I can't help but laugh along, the shared moment of humor bridging the gap between us momentarily. "Fair point. No, we don't."

He leans forward, his demeanor serious. "My men and I, we love your food, Patrick. And when we have business meetings, we prefer not to do them at home. Renting out your place is the best option for privacy and atmosphere."

The logic is sound, and I find myself nodding along. The idea of providing an exclusive experience for Luca Amato and his associates is daunting but not without its perks. "Give me some time to put together a menu and work out a per-person cost. How many will be attending?"

"Let's plan for ten men," he says, already one step ahead.

"Any specific requests for the menu?" I ask, reaching for a notepad.

Luca doesn't hesitate. "Start with those bacon-wrapped scallops as appetizers. They're a hit with my boys."

"Consider it done," I reply, scribbling down notes. The bacon-wrapped scallops are a crowd-pleaser, but ensuring the rest of the menu matches their caliber will be key.

As Luca stands to leave, he hands me a business card. "Get me those numbers, Patrick. I'm looking forward to making this a regular thing."

I watch him leave with a mix of apprehension and excitement. The opportunity to host Luca Amato and his associates once a month could be a boon for Savor, provided I navigate it carefully. The challenge is not only in crafting a menu that impresses Luca but in balancing the demands of a private event with the ethos of my restaurant.

Turning back to my desk, I start jotting down ideas for a menu, my mind already racing with possibilities. This could be a turning point for Savor, a chance to showcase our culinary prowess in a new, albeit unconventional, way.

However, it could also put me squarely in the middle of the mafia's questionable business practices, and I'm not sure what that could entail or if I'm ready to go there.

CHAPTER 11

❧

ALLIE

The next morning, I set off to drop off my resume at Savor. The nerves are there, simmering just under the surface, but excitement's got the upper hand.

Stacy's sprawled on my bed in my room, phone in hand, probably deep into her latest social media spiral, while I'm ransacking my closet for something that screams, 'Hire me; I'm a culinary genius."

"I ran into Caleb yesterday," I blurt out, hoping to distract myself from my pitiful wardrobe.

Stacy barely glances up, her thumbs still flying over her screen. "Caleb?"

I pause, a black blouse in one hand and a beige one in the other. "Tall, dark, and handsome? We dated for, like, a hot minute a while back."

Recognition flickers in Stacy's eyes. Then she laughs. "Oh wait, you mean the *one* guy you've dated. How could I have forgotten?"

"That's the one," I confirm, tossing the black blouse back into the abyss of the closet. "Anyway, he popped up out of nowhere yesterday, all casual like he just happened to be in the neighborhood, and dropped a bombshell: He wants me to meet his dad."

Her interest piqued, Stacy finally puts the phone down. "His dad? Why?"

"Turns out his dad owns Savor, and they're looking for a new sous chef," I say, finally deciding on the beige blouse and black pants.

Stacy sits up, her demeanor shifting from casual observer to full-blown strategist. "Wait, Savor? As in, top-tier, wish-list dining Savor? And he wants you to meet with his dad for a job? Girl, this is huge!"

I can't help the grin that spreads across my face. "I know, right? It's kind of a big deal. Caleb seemed to think I'd be a good fit."

Stacy's suddenly all business. "Okay, we need to make sure you nail this. First impressions are everything, especially with a job like this on the line."

I can't help but feel a surge of gratitude for having Stacy. She's always been my rock, ready to dive head-first into whatever madness comes our way.

She leans back on my bed, a mischievous glint in her eye. "Imagine the money they rake in. Hey, maybe you should give Caleb another shot. Date him again, and you might not even need to work," she jokes, winking exaggeratedly.

I throw a pillow at her, laughing. "Oh, shut it. I'd never do that."

But Stacy's on a roll, not missing a beat. "Or, you know, aim higher. Date the dad! If he owns Savor, you're set for life." Her teasing smile widens as we both burst into laughter at the absurdity of the idea.

After a moment, Stacy turns practical. "Okay, okay, but seriously, let's go shopping. You need to look top-notch for this."

I wince, thinking of all the monthly bills I haven't yet paid. "Rent's due, Stace. I can't really splurge right now. Not to mention, I'm meeting Caleb in an hour."

Undeterred, Stacy jumps to her feet and pulls me toward the closet. "Then let's find something killer from what we already have."

"I've already got an outfit picked out," I say, gesturing to the blouse and slacks draped over my desk chair."

She laughs. "Don't tell me you're planning on dressing for this like it's a job at the damn library. You need something with a little more edge. Come here."

The search turns collaborative, and Stacy runs into her room and returns with a sleek, red, form-fitting dress and a pair of dark red heels. I look at the dress with hesitancy. "Won't this be too tight? I mean, I'm a bit curvier than you."

Stacy gives me a reassuring once-over. "Girl, please. You'll look amazing. Curves are in, and you're going to rock that kitchen interview. Confidence is key."

Her encouragement dispels my doubts, and when I look in the mirror, I have to admit I look good, ready to take on whatever Savor—and Caleb's dad—have in store for me.

Williamsburg is its usual blend of buzzy chic and urban hipness. The neighborhood makes this whole meeting feel like an adventure—like I am on the brink of landing my dream job.

I see Caleb waiting out front as we agreed. He looks almost as eager and giddy as I feel. He spots me and greets me with a hug that lingers just a second too long. It's a bit awkward, and I find myself hoping this connection doesn't lead him to think I want to get back together.

As we break apart, Caleb lays on the charm. "You look great, Allie. Ready to meet my dad?"

I offer a polite smile, sidestepping the flirtation. "Thanks, Caleb. I want to make a good impression."

The restaurant's façade is sleek and stylish, with large glass windows offering a glimpse into the chic interior, where soft lighting and an understated color palette create an inviting atmosphere.

Caleb catches me staring. "Impressive, huh?" he says, a note of pride in his voice.

"It definitely has that wow factor," I reply.

He chuckles. "Just wait until you see the inside. And you know, if you end up working here, you'll be part of the wow."

I laugh nervously. "Let's not get ahead of ourselves."

We make our way through the elegant dining area, and I can't help but feel the eyes of the lunch staff on us. Caleb, seemingly oblivious to the attention, guides me confidently toward the kitchen, where lunch prep is already in full swing.

It's immediately apparent that they run a tight ship because the kitchen looks understaffed. Otherwise, though, it's a chef's dream—state-of-the-art equipment, a spacious prep area, and there's an air of efficiency that speaks volumes about the restaurant's high standards.

As I take it all in, my desire to be part of this team, to stand among these talented individuals, and to contribute my share grows tenfold.

"This kitchen is incredible, Caleb," I whisper in awe as we walk further into it and the moment of truth draws nearer. Caleb knocks on the office door, and a familiar voice calls out, "Come in."

Caleb opens the door and gestures for me to enter first, but I'm so surprised by what I see that I almost stumble. There, seated behind the desk, is Patrick—who, it turns out, is Caleb's father. The realization hits me like a freight train.

I never got Patrick's last name during our date or our dalliance afterward. And we'd never talked about our careers. I suddenly realized how little I knew about the man whom I'd been obsessing over for the past few days.

Patrick doesn't notice me, as his attention is focused on his computer screen, so I take the opportunity to try to compose myself.

"Just a moment," he murmurs, not yet aware of the bombshell standing in his doorway.

My body's reaction to him is immediate. I feel a mix of nerves and desire that I pray isn't written all over my face. I'd prepared myself to meet Caleb's father, the owner of Savor, but not Patrick, the guy I'd slept with only a few nights before.

Finally, he looks up, and our eyes lock. I watch as recognition dawns on him, his expression shifting from professional curiosity to surprise. Smoothly, he rises from his chair, the picture of composure despite the shock.

Caleb, oblivious to the tension, steps forward with a smile. "Dad, this is Allie. Allie, my dad, Patrick Spellman."

Patrick extends his hand, the smile on his face suggesting he's playing along with this "first-time" introduction. "Pleasure to meet you, Allie."

I take his hand, grateful for the charade. It gives me a moment to collect myself, to slip into the role of a chef here for a job, not someone who knows him in a way that's anything but professional. "Thank you, Mr. Spellman. The pleasure is mine."

Internally, I'm a mess. My body remembers how his arms felt around me, the taste of his kiss, the feeling of his cock buried inside of me. It's as if every nerve ending has come alive at the sight of him, a reminder of what we shared.

Caleb looks between us, a hint of confusion in his gaze before he shrugs it off. "I told Dad all about your skills in the kitchen. He's been looking forward to meeting you."

Patrick nods, his attention briefly flitting back to me, an unreadable look in his eyes. "Yes, Caleb's mentioned your work at Verde Oliva. We're eager to see what you might bring to Savor."

I have to force myself to focus on the opportunity at hand, to prove to Patrick why I'm the right choice for the job. But in the back of my mind, the memory of our night together lingers, a tantalizing reminder of the complications that could arise if I take this job.

Yet even under these strange circumstances, one thing is crystal clear—I want him.

CHAPTER 12

PATRICK

I'm thunderstruck. Allie, the woman who's been on my mind the past few days, is here in my office to interview for the sous chef position.

Caleb is beaming, completely oblivious to the undercurrents swirling between us.

"Dad, she's got a magic touch in the kitchen."

Allie's cheeks are dusted with a rosy hue, a sight I find endearing. Is she blushing because of Caleb's compliment, our awkward predicament, or something else?

The situation teeters on the edge of bizarre. "It sounds like you're quite talented," I comment, hoping my tone doesn't give away my apprehension.

Caleb, ever the enthusiastic son, nods vigorously. "Exactly! That's why I knew she'd be perfect for Savor."

The small talk continues, though it does little to alleviate the tension. Eventually, Caleb checks his watch and grimaces. "Ah, crap. I've got to get going. Big day."

When Caleb leaves, I'm left grappling with a mix of emotions. My office suddenly feels confining. There's no place to avoid each other's eyes. I clear my throat, trying to regain some semblance of control over the situation.

The silence stretches between us, becoming an entity of its own until Allie breaks the silence with a rush of words. "I had no idea you were Caleb's dad. Honestly, if I'd known, I probably wouldn't have agreed to come in. I don't want you to think I'm trying to use my connection with Caleb to get this job. I never got your last name the other night."

She looks genuinely concerned, which I find endearing. I chuckle and raise my hand as a way to get her to pause. "Allie, I believe you."

She sighs, and the tension between us eases slightly. "And as for what happened between us, let's just say it has no bearing on your potential role here at Savor. I'm only interested in your talent as a chef."

Allie lets out a breath she seems to have been holding, allowing herself a tight smile. "Thank you. I just want to make sure everything is above board. I'm serious about this job. Cooking is everything to me."

As the initial awkwardness begins to dissipate, our conversation gradually finds its way back to the reason we're both here—to discuss her qualifications for the open sous chef position.

"About that. I'm curious to know how you approach cooking. What's your philosophy in the kitchen?"

Allie leans forward and says with confidence, "For me, cooking is about connecting with ingredients in a way that brings out their best qualities. I like traditional methods of cooking, but I always put an innovative spin on my food while respecting its origins."

Her answer strikes a chord with me, reflecting a depth of understanding and respect for the culinary arts. "That's an admirable approach," I say. "How do you see yourself applying that philosophy here at Savor?"

She smiles, her passion evident. "I've admired Savor, and I feel I could complement and enhance what you've already built here. I'm eager to contribute, to learn from the team, and to push the boundaries of what we can create together."

Listening to her, I'm struck by her sincerity and dedication despite the unexpected way our paths have crossed again. "Let's talk about your experience at Verde Oliva. Working under Marco's leadership can't be easy," I comment, trying to gauge her resilience.

"It's not, but it's taught me a lot about myself and how to thrive in high-pressure situations similar to what exists here at Savor," she responds.

As we talk more about her culinary expertise and the dishes she's created that she's particularly proud of, there's a subtle shift in the atmosphere between us.

"Sounds like you bring a lot of creativity to your cooking. I'm sure that would translate well to Savor's menu."

The compliment seems to warm her, and she leans in slightly, a playful tilt to her lips. "I like to think I bring a little something special to everything I do. Hopefully, that includes my potential role here."

The banter feels natural and easy despite the high stakes of the conversation. "I have no doubt," I respond, allowing a touch of flirtation to color my tone. "It's not just about filling a position, after all. It's about finding someone who fits, who adds to the team in a meaningful way."

Her response is thoughtful, tinged with a lightness that suggests she's picking up on the shift in our dynamic. "I agree," she says thoughtfully, "and I'm not just looking for any kitchen to join. I'm looking for a place where I can really contribute and make a difference. Maybe even spice things up a bit?"

The double entendre hangs between us, charged and playful. I am impressed not just by her culinary talent but also by her ability to hold her own and remain professional.

"Spicing things up is sometimes exactly what a kitchen needs. It keeps everyone on their toes and adds a new dynamic to the dishes."

The ebb and flow of our conversation reveals much about Allie's culinary passion and her aspirations.

Suddenly, her expression shifts as if there's a realization dawning that brings an abrupt pause to our banter. She stands and gathers her things with a courtesy that feels more like a prelude to departure than a simple gesture of politeness. "Thank you for your time, Patrick. I really appreciate it."

I'm taken aback, not ready for the meeting to end, especially on such an uncertain note. "Why are you leaving?" I ask, my concern genuine.

She hesitates, then meets my gaze with a level of honesty that catches me off-guard. "I'm just thinking it might be too awkward working together after ... you know."

The implication hangs heavily in the air, a reminder of our shared night that seemingly neither of us can forget. Acting on impulse, I reach out and rest my hand gently on her arm to halt her retreat.

"Allie, do you really believe I'd hire you just because we shared one night together? Is that the kind of man you think I am?"

Her eyes lock with mine, searching, weighing my sincerity. "No, that's not what I'm saying. It's just ... complicated."

I let out a breath, a mix of frustration and regret coloring my tone. "Look, I'm not that kind of guy. If all you wanted was that one night, then that's all it will ever be."

It kills me to say the words because as I stand there, looking into her eyes, I'm damn sure I want more.

And judging by the way she looks at me, she does, too.

CHAPTER 13

ALLIE

"Jace, double-check the stock for tonight's service," Patrick directs without breaking stride. "Lena, I want those filets to be perfect. Remember, it's as much about the presentation as it is the taste."

As Patrick leads me through the kitchen, his presence commands attention, and the staff responds with the precision of a well-oiled machine.

Observing the dynamic, it's clear that Patrick has mastered the art of leadership. His staff moves with purpose, their dedication evident in every task.

I trail behind him, a flurry of thoughts whirling through my head, chief among them the undeniable attraction I feel toward him—a desire reignited with every moment we're together. Just seeing him in the kitchen is enough to turn me on.

Yet there's a line I'm worried about crossing. The last thing I want is to be seen as the girl who got the job because she slept with the boss and not on my own merits. This is my dream job, and I have to earn it on my own, no matter how complicated my feelings for Patrick might be.

In a moment of boldness or maybe in a desperate attempt to prove myself, I ask, "Would you like to give me a task, a sort of trial to prove I can handle the position?"

"You've worked for Marco for two years?" he asks in response.

I nod.

"Welcome aboard, Allie. If you can handle Marco, I'm pretty sure you'll fit in just fine here. I'm looking forward to seeing what you can do."

Before I can spiral too far into my thoughts, Patrick suddenly shifts into boss mode. I watch as he strides over to one of the younger chefs, who's apparently in the middle of a sauce crisis. It's like stepping into a reality cooking show, minus the dramatic music.

"Let me show you again," Patrick says with authority. "The sauce needs to be velvety, not ... whatever you've managed here."

The young cook, a guy probably not much older than me, looks terrified yet eager to learn. "I thought I followed the recipe exactly, Chef."

Patrick remains patient, grabs a spoon, and switches into teaching mode. "Cooking isn't just about following recipes. It's about intuition, understanding the why behind the what. Watch."

They lean in together, the young cook hanging on to Patrick's every word. There's a master class happening right in front of me, and it's fascinating to watch.

When he's finished, Patrick pats the young man on the shoulder—a gesture that seems to say, "I expect a lot, but I know you can deliver." Turning back to me, his expression hardens. "In this kitchen, it's not just about making food; it's about crafting experiences. Everyone here is crucial to that mission."

I can't help but be impressed. Patrick's tough, but he's also fair. He's worlds apart from Chef Marco, who seems to thrive on fear more than mentoring. Here, when someone is corrected, it's done to educate them and push them to be better.

"Tough but fair. I can work with that," I say, half-joking.

Patrick smirks. There's a hint of challenge in his gaze. "Glad to hear it because I won't go easy on you, either."

We head back to his office to finish our discussion; I mentally give myself a pep talk.

"You'll need to swing by early tomorrow when you can to tackle the mountain of new hire paperwork. Oh, and we'll sort out your uniform," he says, sounding every bit the boss now. "I want you to be ready to start on time."

"Absolutely, I'll be here with bells on," I reply. "Thanks a million, Patrick. This is huge for me. I'll give Marco my two weeks' notice and be ready to roll right after."

He stands, a clear sign that our official business is over, and offers his hand. I hesitate for just a nanosecond because the last time we were this close, paperwork was the last thing on our minds.

Taking his hand causes flashbacks of our night together. Our eyes lock, and suddenly, it's like we're the only two people in the universe. I feel my face flush, and Patrick smirks like he knows the turmoil he's stirring up inside me.

After what feels like an eternity but is probably just a few seconds, I manage to let go of his hand and turn. I throw another thank you over my shoulder and make a beeline for the door.

Stepping outside, I take a moment to collect myself. That's when the reality of what I've just signed on for hits me head-on. How am I supposed to keep my mind on work with Mr. Tall, Dark, and Smoldering hovering over me?

CHAPTER 14

ALLIE

Rushing home with tears in my eyes isn't exactly how I pictured my evening ending.

But here I am, mascara running down my cheeks, all because of Chef Marco's reign of terror.

He swooped in, fork in hand, to pass judgment on my latest creation. He took a bite, and for a second, his eyes lit up like a kid who'd just discovered the joy of popping bubble wrap. But then, he frowned.

"This is all wrong!" he declared, his voice rising over the sizzle and chatter of the kitchen. "The balance is off, the presentation is amateurish, and this ..." he gestured to my dish with the fork, "... this is simply unacceptable."

Maybe it was all in my head, but I could have sworn I saw a dusting of white powder under his nose, evidence that he'd been spending time with his drug of choice.

Before I could muster a defense, he'd tossed my lovingly crafted dish into the trash with all the ceremony of a judge delivering a life sentence. My heart sank to the floor, watching hours of work consigned to the garbage.

But while Marco was deciding that my dish belonged in the trash, a little switch flipped inside me, and I realized I was done. I'd put up with Marco's bullshit for long enough, and now I had a new job. I had prepared to give him two weeks' notice, but at that moment, I had no more fucks to give.

I squared my shoulders and said, "Marco, you're nothing but a bully. You're so scared of a little competition; you'd rather trash good food than admit it's better than anything you've plated in years."

For once, Marco was speechless, and before he could come up with another insult, I said, "I quit! Consider this my notice. Find someone else to push around because I am out of here."

And then I'd stormed out, letting the heavy kitchen door slam behind me. I refused to look back, even though I felt dozens of eyes on me, watching my dramatic exit.

As I stepped outside into the cool night air, my heart was pounding, and I felt a wild mix of fear, relief, and exhilaration. Perhaps I'd just burned my bridges, but I felt freer than I had in years.

Walking away from Marco's kitchen, I couldn't help but think about what the future would hold for me. It was a terrifyingly blank canvas now, but I knew one thing for sure: No one was going to treat me like that ever again.

I'm a whirlwind of emotions as I burst through the door to my apartment. I am teary-eyed but defiant. And to my surprise, the place is empty. No roommates, no dubious smells wafting from the kitchen—just blissful silence.

For a fleeting second, I think, *This is what it would be like to have my own place—no sharing a bathroom, no food disappearing from the fridge.*

I decide to seize the moment. I pour myself a glass of wine from whatever bottle was already open in the fridge and head to the bathroom for a luxurious soak, complete with some fancy bath bombs I've been saving for a special occasion. Because if surviving a showdown with Chef Marco and hurling myself into the unknown isn't special, I don't know what is.

Slipping into the bath, I let the warm water envelop me. The fizzing of each bubble of the bath bomb seems to whisper, "Here's to fresh starts and fiery exits."

I close my eyes, sip my wine, and feel myself start to relax. Savor's kitchen awaits, and with it, a chance to prove that I'm more than just a one-night stand—I'm an excellent chef with hopes and dreams and maybe a dash of boldness.

As the warmth of the bath seeps into my muscles, I let my mind drift toward a fantasy that's been in the back of my mind. My hand slips under the warm water, making its way between my thighs.

The scene unfolds in Savor's kitchen, but it's not the hustle and bustle of a typical day. Instead, it's just Patrick and me alone, the tension between us as palpable.

In this fantasy, I'm at the counter, focusing intently on chopping something. Patrick's overseeing my technique, but the professional critique soon veers into playful banter.

"You sure can handle a knife," he says, a twinkle in his eye, "but can you handle the heat?"

"Oh, I thrive on heat," I quip, my words laced with a double entendre.

The air crackles with tension. Then, as if drawn by some magnetic force, we are face to face. The kitchen fades into the background.

Patrick reaches past me to turn off a burner, his arm brushing against mine, sending a jolt of electricity through me. Our eyes meet, and there's a moment of silent acknowledgment of the intense attraction that's been bubbling just under the surface.

He smiles a cocky grin that says he's fully aware of the effect he's having on me. "Careful, Allie," he whispers, his voice low and husky, "this kitchen isn't just for cooking."

The words hang in the air, charged with the possibility of our flirting becoming something more. My heart races, my breath quickens, and for a fleeting second, the fantasy feels almost real.

"Then what *is* it for?" I ask playfully.

He reaches for me hungrily. "Let me show you."

With that, he pins me against the counter with his hands on either side of me. He's so close I can feel his hardness. I moan and squirm against him.

He leans down and kisses me hard. Even though it's just a fantasy, I can somehow taste his lips and it seems just as real as it did the night we made love. Patrick's got a good eight to ten inches on me, and I have to crane my neck up to meet his lips.

I moan, his hands finding my hips and holding me right where he wants me. His touch makes its way to the buttons of my black chef's coat, undoing them one by one. It's impossibly hot, especially because he's about to make love to me in his own kitchen. The fact that we're about to do it someplace we most definitely shouldn't makes the fantasy that much hotter.

I undo the buttons of his shirt, exposing his white T-shirt, which strains against his muscled shoulders and chest. There's something irresistible about seeing him in that tight T-shirt and those black pants, knowing he's about to take me in his domain.

I moan in the tub, my leg draped over the side, water dripping onto the mat. My hips are angled in such a way that I can rub my clit just how I need to in order to rush to a quick climax. I'm alone for the moment, but it's only a matter of time before one or more of my roommates return and need to use the bathroom.

I push those boring, real-life concerns to the back of my mind and return to the fantasy. Chef Patrick has my chef's coat off and his hands are under the sleeveless undershirt I have on beneath. His fingers slip under my bra, and he takes hold of my breasts.

"Do you have any idea how hard it is to ignore you when you're here in my kitchen?" he asks as his lips roam my neck and hands knead my breasts. "Do you know how much time I spend thinking of fucking you just like this?"

All I can do is moan. He's so hard, and it's unfair that he's not inside of me. Patrick rubs his cock over my pussy before lifting me onto the countertop. He grinds against me, his manhood pressing against my clit through my pants.

"Stop teasing me," I say, my fingers working through his hair as he plants kisses along my collarbone. "Just take me."

"Just take me *what?*" he asks, pulling my shirt over my head.

"Just take me, please, Chef."

He grins, and I know I've given the right answer.

With that, he removes my pants and underwear, and I feel the cool stainless-steel countertop cool against my bare ass. I return the favor, yanking down his pants, his cock leaping out into my hand. He feels perfect to the touch.

"You're so hard," I say, stroking his length.

"Hard for you," he replies, leaning in and nibbling my earlobe, "so fucking hard for you."

I take him by the base and place his cock at the entrance to my slit. But when I attempt to guide him inside, he pauses.

"Something wrong?" I ask.

He backs slowly from me.

"Where are we right now?"

I'm confused. "In your kitchen?"

He nods slowly, a sexy-as-fuck, wolfish grin on his lips.

"That's right. My kitchen. And in my kitchen, we obey my rules."

I swallow. He's back to being the boss.

"And what rules might those be?"

"Rule one." He raises a single finger. "You do what I say. Understood?"

"Understood, Chef."

Another grin.

"Hop off the counter."

I do as he asks and stand in front of him. He looks up and down at my naked body with an appraising glance as if I'm the kitchen's daily meat delivery and he's checking its quality.

"God, you're fucking sexy."

The pressure between my legs is so intense that I can hardly focus on his words.

"Turn around."

I do as he asks.

"Bend over and grab the counter."

Again, I do as he asks. I start to turn to look at him but only manage a quick glance before he orders, "Keep your eyes forward."

Again, I obey.

"Do you see the spatula on the wall ahead? The one with the red rubber end?"

I spot it. "Yes."

"Yes, what?"

"Yes, Chef."

"Grab it and give it to me."

In the blink of an eye, I feel the sensation of the cool metal against my ass.

Then, before I can react, he spanks me on one cheek with it. I feel the sting, but I don't react; it's kind of exhilarating.

Before I can stop him, he spanks me on the other cheek. A perfect blend of pain and pleasure rushes through me. He then places the corner of the spatula against my lower back and trails it up my spine. The feel of the cool metal makes me shiver.

"How does that feel?" he asks. "Do you like it when I'm rough with you?"

"Yes," The word shoots out of me before I have a chance to realize what I'm saying.

But it's true. I love it.

He sets the spatula down gently on the counter. Then he penetrates me with his cock at my opening and pushes inside. I'm so freaking wet that his thrust into me is totally effortless. He glides inside and stretches me out with his thickness, bottoming out in an instant.

Back in the real world, I hear the telltale sound of the front door opening, followed by the chatter of roommates, which brings me back to reality.

Shit.

Someone comes to the bathroom and pulls the handle. Thankfully, I'd remembered to lock it.

"Hey, you in there?" asks Myra.

My eyes flash, my hand still on my pussy.

"Um, yeah! Two seconds!"

I push myself back into the fantasy, imagining Patrick driving hard into me over and over, his hips crashing against mine, his hands on my sides. He spanks me again and again, and soon, an orgasm is ripping through me.

It's more intense than I'd been expecting, and I have to grab the towel and bite down hard on it, the thick fabric muffling my shouts of total pleasure. The orgasm fades, and I'm done, totally spent, my leg limply hanging over the side of the tub.

The knob jangles again.

"Come on!" Myra whines. "I really have to pee!"

"Almost done!"

I hop out of the tub and dry off, wrapping a towel around myself before opening the door. Myra blows past me into the bathroom. I hurry into my room and sit down on the bed, the fantasy still fresh in my mind.

CHAPTER 15

PATRICK

The moment Allie strides into Savor's kitchen, it's impossible not to notice her. She's dressed in jeans, a T-shirt, and a jacket. She wears a pair of clunky black kitchen shoes on her feet.

God, she looks so fucking good. My cock stiffens at the sight of her, and I have to force myself to get a grip. There has to be a professional line, clear and non-negotiable. I'm the boss here, not some lovestruck fool. Mixing business with pleasure is not going to happen. She's here to work, and my job is to lead, not to get tangled up in desire.

As she approaches, gratitude in her eyes as she once again thanks me for the opportunity, I decide to address the elephant in the room and tell her that I heard through the culinary grapevine about her untimely exit from Marco's before she'd called to let me know she could start immediately and not in two weeks as we'd originally discussed.

I greet her before leading her into my office. "Listen, Allie," I say. "I understand the frustration of working under someone like Marco, but I need to make one thing crystal clear—the kind of confrontation you had with him won't fly here."

I pause, making sure she grasps the gravity of my statement. "I'm the owner and executive chef, and Savor is my domain. Respect and discipline will be maintained in the kitchen at all times. If you're going to thrive here, you need to fall in line and follow my lead. Understand?"

She reacts with a mix of surprise and acknowledgment. "Of course, Chef. I have nothing but respect for what you've built here."

"Good," I say, nodding. "Your talent got you through the door, but it's your performance that will determine whether or not you stay. You've got a lot to prove, not just to me but to everyone in this kitchen."

She stands there stunned as I look for a spot for her. "Prep work." I gesture to a pile of onions that need dicing. "You can start there. I'll check in on you in a bit. Sarah will be around to answer any questions."

"Of course, Chef," she says.

With that, I stride to the other side of the kitchen.

Placing Allie's workstation as far away from mine as possible wasn't just a strategic move; it was a necessity. The closer she is, the harder it will be for me to concentrate.

I catch myself listening in as Sarah, our current sous chef who's soon to be on maternity leave, starts to fill Allie in. Even from a distance, I feel Allie's presence.

"Remember, timing is everything here," Sarah explains, her voice carrying the weight of experience and the clarity of someone who's navigated many a service under intense pressure.

Allie responds immediately. "What's the best way to keep the line moving smoothly during a rush?" she asks. "Are there any specific signals or cues I should be aware of?"

Her question is smart, pinpointing one of the critical aspects of kitchen efficiency. Sarah offers a detailed explanation, but I find myself interjecting, unable to resist the opportunity to engage. "Eye contact and clear communication," I call out from my station across the room. "There's no room for ambiguity when orders are piling up."

Allie turns toward me and nods in acknowledgment. "Understood. And when it comes to plating, is there a standard presentation for each dish, or is there some room for creative interpretation?"

"Always follow our standard," I reply, my tone leaving no room for doubt, "but creativity that enhances, not distracts, is always welcome. If you can first show me that you understand the dish, then you can try to make it yours."

I turn back to my work but still listen while Allie and Sarah delve deeper into their culinary discussion.

"In this kitchen, your ability to experiment while preserving the dish's soul is what will distinguish you," I hear Sarah say.

"Gotcha," Allie says, grateful and poised. "I'm here to absorb, contribute, and innovate where and when I can."

Her exchange with Sarah confirms my instinct about her. She has a spark that will enhance our culinary approach. However, it's her allure that's more of a distraction.

Memories from our night together continue to invade my thoughts. The way her aura filled the room, the softness of her skin, and the look in her eyes—it all floods back, vivid and unsettling.

Suddenly, she laughs, which causes my hand to slip and nearly ruin the prep work in front of me.

"Everything all right, Chef?" one of the line cooks asks, cocking an eyebrow at me.

"I'm fine," I retort, a bit more sharply than necessary, mentally berating myself for losing my focus during the rush of lunch service.

However, as the shift continues, I can't help but let my gaze wander to Allie as she gets into the rhythm of our kitchen. Her movements are precise and confident, unlike the typical newcomer's. She's in her element—handling orders in coordination with the team and executing dishes with expertise. I'm impressed but also a little irked, given the internal conflict she stirs within me.

As the lunch service concludes and the kitchen transitions into dinner prep, I find a moment of quiet to consider Allie's first day. Her performance was remarkable, and her impact was immediate. Despite the personal complications, she's proven herself an indispensable part of the team already.

"Chef, everything okay?" asks the same line cook as before when he notices I'm lost in thought.

"Yeah, I'm fine. Just focus on the prep for dinner service," I snap, redirecting my attention to the tasks at hand.

Later, I notice that Allie is getting ready to leave. She's changed out of her chef's coat and is dressed in a simple T-shirt and jeans, the same thing she was wearing the other night.

I catch up to her before she can leave to acknowledge her exemplary work. "You did a fine job today, Allie. You fit in better than I hoped," I say. "You keep this up; you might have a future here."

She turns to face me, and before I can filter my thoughts, I find myself saying, "You look really good in jeans." Then I catch myself. "I'm sorry. That was unprofessional."

She flushes in embarrassment. "It's all right, Chef. No harm done."

For a moment longer than what professionalism dictates, our gazes lock, a silent acknowledgment of the unspoken tension that's been simmering between us. It's a moment fraught with the potential for more, a promise of what could be if not for the boundaries we both know we need to maintain.

Just then, Sarah interrupts us to say goodbye. "Great job today, Allie," she says, unaware of what was happening between us.

As I turn to respond to Sarah with a smile and a few parting words, Allie uses the opportunity to slip away, her departure a silent concession to the complexity of our situation. Watching her go, I can't help but think it's a smart move. The pull between us is undeniable and magnetic, and keeping a respectful distance feels increasingly like a Herculean effort, like the hardest—and best—thing to do.

CHAPTER 16

ALLIE

"Table five, I need two lambs and three sea bass, and make it quick!" Patrick demands, his voice firm and unwavering.

Around me, the team responds in a perfectly timed chorus, "Yes, Chef!" The unity, the respect—it's all so captivating.

The dinner shift at Savor hits like a tidal wave, the front bustling with energy, the back a symphony of disciplined chaos. And then there's Patrick, the conductor of this frenzied orchestra, his commands cutting through the air with the precision of a seasoned general.

Amidst the flurry, I find myself grappling with my thoughts about him. There's no denying he's got that rugged charm, his culinary genius is off the charts, and yet, he's got this sternness that's worlds apart from the man I thought I knew outside these kitchen walls.

"Patrick's like a whole different beast in here, huh?" I whisper to Sarah, who's beside me, plating a dish with meticulous care.

She glances up, a knowing smile on her face. "You mean you're surprised he's no longer the charming prince once the heat's on? Welcome to Savor, where the chef is as sharp as his knives."

I chuckle, my gaze drifting back to Patrick. Unlike Marco, who often allowed his own genius to get in his way, Patrick is a beacon of control and clarity.

"I mean, Marco had his moments, but Patrick? He's on another level—like he was born for this."

Sarah nods, her focus never wavering from her task. "Patrick doesn't just run the kitchen; he *is* the kitchen."

As I watch him, I feel more than just professional admiration; it's deeper, more primal. Seeing how he commands the room, dictating orders with such a calm, assertive presence ... it's, well, hot. The truth of the matter is that I've spent half the shift totally wet.

As the night wears on, with each "Yes, Chef!" echoing through the kitchen, my fascination with Patrick only grows. We are in the thick of service, yet my thoughts are consumed by him—his leadership, his vision, and, dare I say, the intensity.

During a brief lull in the action, I jokingly say, "So, Patrick, does barking orders come naturally to you, or is it a skill you've honed over the years?"

He shoots me a hard look, but there's a hint of amusement in his eyes. "Allie, just focus on your dishes," he says in all seriousness, not my command style," he retorts.

The smile leaves my lips, and as I turn back to my work, I cast a glance toward Sarah who's still smashing it, even though she's eight months pregnant and standing on her feet for hours can't be easy for her.

"Sarah, you sure you're all right?" I ask, catching her during a split-second breather.

She shoots me a look that could curdle milk. "I'm fine, Allie," she snaps back, but it's clear she's anything but.

Moments later, Sarah winces as she narrowly avoids cutting herself. Leaning toward her, I say, "Seriously, talk to me. You look like you're on your last legs."

She sighs, finally admitting she's wiped out, "My feet could be mistaken for balloons at this point."

Without hesitation, I dash over to Patrick, concern fueling my sprint. "Chef, we've got a situation with Sarah. She can barely stand, and she's clearly in a lot of discomfort."

Patrick's gaze softens as he looks toward Sarah, his tough-as-nails exterior melting just a tad. "Sarah, you're benched. Go home," he declares, with the kind of firmness that brooks no argument.

Sarah, ever the warrior, tries to protest. "But Chef, I can—"

Patrick cuts her off. the caring side of him making a rare appearance in the kitchen. "No buts. Your health comes first. We'll manage."

As Sarah reluctantly agrees to leave, the reality of the situation hits me like a poorly made soufflé—her workload is now my workload. " I guess it's showtime for me," I say, half to myself, bracing for the onslaught.

Patrick throws me an encouraging yet challenging look. "You've got the skills. Just stay focused, and you'll be fine," he says and walks away. That's when I realize I either had to sink or swim.

As I juggle Sarah's duties on top of my own, adrenaline and sheer willpower take over.

"Keep the magic happening, Tucker!" Patrick shouts over the clatter, his encouragement a lifeline in the storm.

Despite the exhaustion threatening to set in, there's a thrill in the chaos, a buzz in proving that I can indeed keep up with the best of them. As the night wears on, and with every plate that leaves the kitchen, I realize this is exactly where I'm meant to be.

Jumping from the newbie pool straight into the deep end isn't easy, and despite my best efforts not to drown in orders, I start to fall behind.

Patrick swoops in to see why his new sous chef is floundering. "Tucker, you're holding up the damn show. Let's get those dishes moving," he demands, every inch the boss. Each time he gets close to me, I catch a whiff of his scent, a mix of cologne and kitchen spice.

Then, he accidentally brushes my arm, and it sends a shockwave through me. "Sorry," he mumbles, stepping back as if he had touched a hot stove. Our eyes lock, and the air crackles with the electricity between us.

But it's Friday night, and there's no time for long, lingering looks. We break eye contact, diving back into our work, but the moment stays with me, albeit in the back of my mind.

Despite the relentless pace, that accidental touch and the tension-filled apology fuel me through the evening, adding an extra sizzle to my step.

As plates fly out and the kitchen buzzes with energy, I can't help but feel a thrill. Between dodging flames and Patrick's eagle-eye supervision, I'm proving I've got what it takes and then some. The night's a blur of flavors, fires, and fleeting touches, each moment building on the last, creating a heady mix of professional pride and personal interest. Patrick calls out over the clamor, his earlier sternness giving way to a hint of something that feels more intimate. "Great recovery, Tucker. Keep that fire burning,"

Who would've thought that a pressure-cooker environment could be such an aphrodisiac? But I'm slicing, dicing, and simmering in more ways than one, all under the watchful gaze of Savor's culinary king.

The kitchen is crazy busy, but I'm giving it my all, tossing everything I've got into the mix. When the last order finally goes out and the kitchen's frenetic pace eases, I feel exhilarated. I lean against the counter to catch my breath, my gaze drifting over to Patrick, who is plating something that looks incredible.

Curiosity wins out over exhaustion, so I meander over, not wanting to miss a chance to learn from the master. But when I draw near, he throws me an irritated look and says, "I don't particularly enjoy an audience hovering over me while I'm working."

"Sorry, Chef," I mutter quick on the apology and slowly move away. "I just couldn't help but be curious about what culinary magic you're conjuring up."

He pauses, then perhaps sensing my genuine interest, begins to describe the dessert with a passion I wasn't expecting. "It's a deconstructed lemon tart," he explains, his hands moving with precision and grace that's utterly captivating. "Instead of a traditional presentation, I've separated the elements to play with the textures and flavors."

I'm hooked as I watch in awe as he zests a lemon with the finesse of a seasoned artist. His technique is flawless, and his focus is unwavering.

"That sounds incredible," I say, genuinely impressed by the creativity and thought he put into the dish. "I mean, who thinks to deconstruct a lemon tart?"

He cracks a rare smile, pleased with my interest. "Only someone trying to push the boundaries of traditional dessert," he quips, his earlier annoyance seemingly forgotten in the shared moment of culinary appreciation.

As he plates the final component, I can't help but marvel at the beauty of it all—the dish, the dedication, and, yes, maybe the chef as well.

"You make it look so easy," I say, my tone laced with admiration and a hint of playfulness. Patrick chuckles, a sound that warms me. "Well, it takes practice, Tucker. Lots of it," he replies, offering me a glimpse of the hard work behind his effortless skill.

"You don't have any food allergies, do you?" Patrick suddenly asks.

Caught off guard, I blink up at him. "Uh, nope. All clear on that front." Then, before the words fully land, Patrick's already in motion. With the grace of a magician pulling a rabbit out of a hat, he scoops up a bit of his masterpiece and, in one fluid motion, presents the spoonful of dessert like an offering, holding it out for me to taste. The flavors explode in my mouth.

"That's incredible," I say once I've managed to collect myself. "Is this what you whip up when you're bored?"

He chuckles again, a sound that sends a delightful shiver down my spine. "Just something I've been playing around with," he admits.

It's so ridiculously good that I'm momentarily worried my knees might give out. How does one stand after such a culinary revelation? But then, Patrick's gaze shifts past me, landing on the aftermath of my dinner service hustle—to my workstation, which currently looks like a disaster zone.

"Looks like you've got your work cut out for you before you leave," he observes, the hint of a smirk playing at the corners of his mouth.

Heat floods my cheeks as I glance back at my war zone. "Yeah, things got a bit explosive in the heat of the moment," I quip, already mourning the loss of my brief moment in dessert heaven.

He surveys the chaos with a critical eye, then locks eyes with me again. "But you kept up. That's what counts. I'll let the mess slide—this time."

He turns and strides away, and my heart does flip-flops, not just from the taste of that lemon tart but from the thrill of earning Patrick's nod of approval—even if it comes with a hint of a reprimand for making a mess.

Armed with a dishcloth and a newfound zest (pun totally intended), I tackle my station. But cleaning somehow feels less like a chore and more like the rewarding aftermath of a successful performance. Patrick's parting words, "this time," echo in my mind. It's like he's challenging me, and I'm more than ready to accept.

As I scrub and sort, I can't help but look forward to my next shift. If I can survive nights of kitchen chaos with Patrick occasionally feeding me bites of dessert, then there's a lot to look forward to.

After a while, I scrub away, lost in thoughts of lemon tarts and lingering glances; I realize I'm the last one left in the kitchen. Patrick is probably buried in paperwork in his office, which presents a dilemma. Patrick's rule is that no one walks to their car or the train station alone. It's a safety thing, and it's much appreciated. But after the charged atmosphere between us all evening, I'm hesitant to knock on his door. Yet the thought of navigating the dark streets by myself scares me, so I find myself outside his office, knocking softly on the open door.

Stepping inside, I catch him in mid-thought, his intense focus shifting to me. That familiar jolt of connection zaps through the air, making the room feel smaller and warmer. "Everything okay?" he asks. His voice is smooth yet laced with mild concern.

I'm suddenly hyper-aware of the small yet charged space between us. "Uh, everyone's gone, and I was wondering if you could walk me to the station," I manage, feeling oddly vulnerable yet bold under his gaze.

He stands and closes the distance between us with a few measured steps. Instead of heading for the door, he stops just a hair's breadth away, invading my personal space with the ease of a man used to getting what he wants. "Allie," he starts, his voice low, "I've been wanting to do this all night, all week, actually."

His confession hangs in the air, a tantalizing promise, and my heart's doing acrobatics, and suddenly, it's like we're the only two people in the world. The air around snaps with anticipation, with want. I don't need any more encouragement. Throwing caution to the wind, I stand on my tiptoes and meet his lips, and it's like lighting the fuse on a bottle rocket. Everything feels right. Reckless, maybe, but oh-so right.

CHAPTER 17

PATRICK

In the shadowed quiet of my office, everything else fades into the background, leaving just Allie and me. Our lips lock, and we kiss deeply, revealing secrets we hadn't yet spoken aloud.

I carefully peel her chef's jacket from her shoulders, the fabric falling to the floor, heightening the anticipation between us. The heat from the ovens lingers, mingling with the faint scent of citrus and her unique floral fragrance, intoxicating in its subtlety.

Her skin is warm and smooth under my touch as I trace the curve of her arms, pulling her closer. She fits against me perfectly, her body a natural extension of my own. As her breath quickens, it stirs the air around my neck, each exhale a spark against my skin.

"We're making more than just dinner tonight, aren't we?" I murmur as our movements sync in a slow, deliberate dance. She laughs softly, the sound mixing with the hum of the refrigeration units—our own private soundtrack.

"In a kitchen full of spices, you're the most intoxicating one," I quip, feeling her smile against my lips.

She pulls back slightly, a playful glint in her eye. "Really, Patrick? Do you use that line to get your soufflés to rise? Lucky for you I'm already smitten," she teases.

I laugh, loving the way she never lets me get too serious, not even in my own domain. "Well, it works; what can I say?" I counter, my hands finding the small of her back, drawing her closer as we both begin to slip out of the remaining barriers of our chef's uniforms.

Soon, we're down to nothing but our underwear. She looks so fucking hot in her white thong and matching bra. My cock turns as solid as the stainless-steel counter, and I want to devour her like a meal.

She's feeling extra bold, however, and steps forward. She's hungry, and I can tell there's only one thing in this kitchen that'll satisfy her.

I run my hand up her thigh, finding the moisture between her legs.

"Oh, oh, God." The words escape from her mouth the moment I make contact.

I rub her pussy gently through her panties, the fabric already soaked. All I can think about is how she might taste. I slip my fingers underneath the elastic and slide them into the slick, wet folds of her pussy.

Her eyes flash for a moment, and then she bucks against my hand. I guide her back, pushing her into a sitting position on the counter, and spread her legs open wide. Allie arches her back and moans as I finger her. She's wet as hell, her tight warmth gripping me.

I kiss her hard, and my tongue finds the same rhythm as my fingers. She reaches behind me and grabs my hair, holding me in place, making sure I don't move an inch.

I keep fingering her, feeling her pussy clench around my fingers, listening to the soft pants and moans that fill the air.

"You're close," I say. "Come for me. Right now."

She nods, barely, then releases. Her whole body tightens at once, then relaxes.

"Patrick!" she cries out as she comes.

I keep fingering her through the orgasm, the sight of her unraveling making me so hard I can barely think straight. As the climax wanes, all I can think about is giving her more.

She opens those gorgeous eyes, and I reach around to unclasp her bra. Allie's round, gorgeous tits fall out, and I waste no time licking and sucking her nipples, savoring that lovely saltiness.

"That was amazing," she says as I toss the bra aside.

"Good, but I'm not done with you yet."

One of her eyebrows raises. "Is that right?"

"That's right. Now, turn around."

She flashes me a sly grin, and I can sense she's wondering what's on my mind. But Allie complies, hopping off the counter and turning. I grab her hips, pulling her back against me, pressing my hardness to her ass.

"You feel that?" I ask. "You feel how turned on you make me?"

She's moaning, squirming against my cock.

"Yes, I do."

"Tell me what you want, gorgeous."

She bites her lip, still squirming against me.

Her response is without hesitation. "I want you inside of me."

I chuckle. "I bet you do." I take my hands from her hips and step back. "Now, lean forward and grab the counter."

She complies and bends her gorgeous body forward at the hips, slowly taking hold of the counter. I take in the sight of her perfect, round ass, her pink slit glistening for me. It takes all the self-control I have not to step forward and bury myself to the hilt inside of her.

"Then you're going to have to be a good girl. Can you be a good girl for me?"

"Yes, I can."

I place my left hand on her hip and spank her right cheek. She shutters and moans from the action. "Do you like that?" I ask her.

"Yes, yes I do," she confirms.

I spank her again, watching her ass shake as she tilts her head upward and arches her back in pleasure. I repeat the same on her left cheek, and she moans even louder. By this point, I can't hold back any longer. I need to be buried inside of her, and I need to feel her tightness gripping me. She's glistening with a thin sheen of sweat, her chest expanding and contracting.

I take my cock by the base, placing it at her entrance. She's soaking wet, the spanking clearly having done its job. I can't resist dropping down to my knees, spreading her lips, and burying my face in her pussy, sucking and tasting her.

God, she's fucking delicious. I grin a bit at the irony. I'm in the best kitchen in New York, yet all I want to eat is *her*.

She moans, pushing back into my face, letting me know that I'm giving her what she craves.

I rise back up, wiping my mouth with the back of my hand, her sweetness lingering on my lips.

I push into her slowly, letting her adjust to my size. She gasps hard, her body tensing as I enter her. My cock slides effortlessly into her slick folds, and soon I'm completely buried.

She feels so perfect, so fucking good.

I pull back and drive back in.

"Mm ..." The noise flows from her, and as she turns her head to look back at me, I can see a sly smile of total bliss form on her plush lips.

I keep my hands on the sexy curves of her hips, holding Allie right where I want her as I feel her pussy slide up and down my length. I bury myself deep again and again, the sounds of my body colliding with hers sounding throughout the kitchen's stillness.

Together, we create a perfect rhythm as I crash into her, and she pushes herself back into me. She's moaning and panting; my heart's pounding hard.

"Just like that," she begs. "Just like that, please."

I'm getting close to the point of no return. I glance down, watching my cock push into her again and again. As she arches with impending orgasm, I reach up and grab a handful of her blonde curls, pulling her head back just enough to give her that perfect blend of pleasure and pain.

"Are you ready to come for me?" I ask.

"Yes, so ready."

"Then ask for permission."

My pace is relentless, and my self-control is vanishing by the moment. All I want to do is explode inside of her.

But not until I get my answer.

"Please. Please let me come."

And that's all I need. I thrust into her, and her pussy clenches hard one last time. I release, and so does she, my cock pulsing inside of her as I drain completely. I feel the heat of my cum as her tightness milks me dry.

I grunt hard, and she screams with wild abandon. Coming with her, rising together, brings everything to another level.

My legs are shaking as I finish and slide my cock out of her, a bit of my seed trickling out. I scoop my arm underneath her, turning her around and bringing her against me. She gazes up at me with those sexy eyes, and I can't resist kissing her slowly, deeply.

"That was nice," she says with a coy smile.

CHAPTER 18

ALLIE

"Are you okay?"

As we lay on the plush rug covering the cool, hard floor of his office, basking in the quiet aftermath of our escapade, I feel a glow radiating from within. It's like I'm wrapped in a soft, warm blanket made of pure bliss.

"I'm more than okay," I breathe out, still caught in the haze of pleasure.

His rich and resonant laughter fills the room. "What about dessert?" he asks, his voice tinged with a hint of naughtiness.

The suggestion spikes my heart rate again, curiosity mingling with possibilities. "I'd really like that," I reply, propping myself up on one elbow to look at him better. "But I think for tonight, I should probably head home."

He nods, a smile playing on his lips as he extends his hand to help me up. "Of course. Let's get you home safe and sound," he says as we both stand and put on our clothing, trying to look somewhat presentable after our little kitchen rendezvous.

"So, is this your standard post-service routine, Chef?" I tease, fiddling with my shirt.

Patrick flashes a sly grin, expertly buttoning up his chef's jacket. "Only when the evening's performance is exceptionally noteworthy," he replies, his eyes sparkling with mischief.

We share a chuckle, but as I slip into my shoes, a sobering realization cuts through the laughter. Here I am, caught up with a man who's not only my boss but also my ex's dad. The joy of the moment starts to feel a tad weighted.

Noticing my sudden quiet, Patrick's expression shifts to concern. "Everything all right?" he asks, closing the gap between us with a few steps.

I force a smile, attempting to brush off the seriousness. "Just thinking about the muscle ache I'll have tomorrow from tonight's workout," I jest, but the smile that follows doesn't quite mask my unease.

He doesn't miss a beat, though. Stepping closer, he gently lifts my chin with his fingers, ensuring I meet his eyes. "Allie, what's really on your mind?" he asks, his tone gentle yet probing.

His straightforward concern and the tender way he touches me make my heart both swoon and sink. He's so direct, so genuine, it strips away any pretense. "It's a bit much, you know?" I confess, letting the words tumble out. "You're amazing, Patrick, and what's happening between us is definitely something electric. But you're also my boss. And Caleb's dad. It's kind of a lot to juggle."

He listens intently, his thumb softly caressing my jawline. "I get it, and I never want you to feel pressured or uncomfortable. We can take things slow, step by step. I want you to feel safe with me," he reassures me. His voice is as comforting as a warm cup of cocoa on a snowy day.

That earnestness, that promise of patience, does things to my heart. "Thanks. I really appreciate that." I respond. My voice is soft, my defenses melting a bit more with his every word.

As we prepare to make our way out, a whirlwind of doubts starts to swirl in my mind. What if I'm reading all this wrong? What if this incredible connection is just temporary?

He places his hand on the small of my back, a gesture that makes me feel so damn good I could cry. But I play it cool.

He studies me for a moment, his concern palpable. "Are you sure you're okay to take the train home?" he asks. I'm not entirely accustomed to his protective tone of voice. "I can always drop you off."

I manage a laugh, though it comes out a bit strained. "Yeah, I promise. I'm good, really," I insist, trying to inject a bit of lightness into the conversation. It's been a while since anyone apart from Stacy has shown this kind of concern for me, and it feels both strange and heartwarming.

"All right, just making sure," he says, giving me a gentle smile that makes me want to spill all my fears and hopes right there. But I hold back, clinging to my self-protective instincts.

Patrick grabs his keys and gestures for me to follow. "I like to do a final walk-through every night," he explains as we stroll through the dimly lit restaurant, his presence comforting in the vast, quiet space.

"Every night? That's dedication," I remark, watching him expertly navigate between tables and chairs.

"Yeah," he nods, checking each section with a practiced eye. "Gotta make sure everything's perfect for tomorrow."

Curious, I lean a little closer. "And what happens if it's not?"

He gives me a half-smile, the dim lighting casting intriguing shadows across his face. "Then I handle it. It could mean a stern chat the following day with whoever was in charge. I've been here until two a.m. once or twice."

"Really? That late?" I tease, bumping his shoulder lightly with mine. "Sounds like a wild night."

He laughs, a rich sound that fills the quiet around us. "Oh, it's wild, all right. Just me and the contents of the walk-in."

As we reach the front door, he does a final lock check and sets the alarm. "Part of the charm of owning a place like this," he adds, his tone light but sincere.

"I'm impressed," I say as we step outside into the cool night air. "It's more than just running the kitchen, isn't it? You really take care of everything."

"Absolutely," he agrees. "It's all about the details and part of being an owner."

As the cool night wraps around us, I find myself not wanting the conversation to end. "Thanks for the late-night tour," I say, my voice playful.

He chuckles, meeting my gaze. "My pleasure."

"Owning a place like Savor is kind of a dream of mine," I confess, tucking a loose strand of hair behind my ear. "But it feels like it's light-years away."

Patrick glances over; his eyes are thoughtful under the streetlights. "I wouldn't say that. From what I've seen, you've got the smarts and the talent to make it happen," he replies earnestly. His compliment sends a warm flush through me,

His words transports me to cloud nine, and I realize how much his opinion matters to me. I try to play it cool, to keep my excitement under wraps, but it bubbles up irresistibly.

"Thanks. That means a lot coming from you."

We reach the subway station. "Goodnight, Allie," he says, his voice a soft rumble that reverberates through my spinning senses.

I watch him walk away; every step he takes leaves a mark on the night and on my heart. Left standing there, bathed in starlight and the lingering warmth of his lips, I know I'm in trouble.

Big, delightful trouble.

CHAPTER 19

ALLIE

The next few weeks at Savor whirl by like a hurricane, with Patrick and me sneaking moments whenever we can. Our rendezvous spots are limited to the hidden nooks and crannies of the kitchen because my place is out—thanks to my ever-present roommates—and his is a definite no-go with Caleb in the apartment next door.

Each encounter is more electric than the last, leaving me breathless and increasingly curious about Patrick's deeper layers. He had introduced me to a dash of BDSM a while back, just a hint, really, but since then, nothing. Part of me wonders if he's holding back, worried about scaring me off.

I'm not scared; I'm intrigued. Seriously intrigued.

As each day ticks by, my curiosity about those unexplored adventures builds. It's like standing in front of a mystery dish covered with a silver dome: you don't know exactly what's under there, but you just know it's going to be good. Or at least interesting.

I'm chopping vegetables one quiet morning before the rush, pondering whether or not I should ask Patrick about his "special menu items" in the bedroom concerning BDSM.

Later, as we're both prepping for the lunch service, I lean closer to him, my voice low. "Hey, Chef, remember that little culinary experiment you shared a few weeks back?" I start, trying to keep it light yet direct.

Patrick looks up from his meticulous dicing, a flicker of something undefinable crossing his features. "Yes, I remember," he replies, his tone careful.

I take a deep breath, tossing the vegetables into a sizzling pan before continuing. "I was wondering if you might be planning to explore that menu further because I've been reading up on those dishes, and they sound quite diverse and flavorful."

He chuckles, then says, "Flavorful, huh?" He wipes his hands on a towel, turning to face me fully. "I didn't want to push you into anything you're not ready for."

I meet his gaze, my determination simmering alongside the onions. "Consider me ready for a taste test. I'm curious, and let's be honest—I trust you with all of the kitchen knives around here, so I think I can trust you with this, too."

His smile then is slow and full of promises. "All right," he agrees, "let's plan a proper exploration. But outside of work hours, and definitely not in the kitchen."

"Deal," I say quickly, excitement zipping through me like lightning.

Later, as I slip into the bathroom for a quick break, Liz, one of the waitresses, hurries in, looking a bit frantic. "Hey,

Allie, you wouldn't happen to have a tampon, would you?" she asks, her voice edged with desperation.

"Sure thing," I reply, reaching into my work bag and handing her one from the small makeup bag I keep stocked with essentials.

"You're a lifesaver," Liz sighs in relief, her gratitude genuine.

As she thanks me, I find myself staring down into the open bag, frowning. The realization hits me suddenly, stark and a bit unnerving. I haven't reached for anything in this bag for myself in longer than I care to admit.

My mind races, the implications spinning out before me, and suddenly, the playful banter and the worries about Caleb finding out about us seem to fade into the background against the new, pressing concerns popping up in my mind.

Back at my chopping station, I'm slicing and dicing, but my mind's working through a whole different kind of problem. I realize I haven't been as consistent with the pill as I should have been, what with starting the new job and the excitement of sneaking around with Patrick.

I shake my head, attempting to clear it of the spiral that's sure to come. I need to focus on work and figure the rest out after my shift. I'll stop on my way home and grab a pregnancy test.

There's no use worrying about it until I know for sure what's going on.

Back in the familiarity of my own apartment after work, I'm buzzing from the evening's unexpected turns.

I kick off my shoes and slump onto the couch beside Stacy. The kitchen adrenaline is fading, replaced by gnawing anxiety about the pregnancy test burning a hole in my purse. Stacy's eyes are on the TV, but she senses the shift in my energy instantly.

"Hey, what's up? You look like you just witnessed a murder," she says, muting the TV and turning to face me.

I hesitate, the words heavy on my tongue. "I might be overreacting, but I'm a bit worried," I start, my voice exhausted.

Stacy's expression softens, her attention fully on me now. "About what? Is everything okay with the job, with Patrick?"

I let out a shaky laugh, pulling the small box from my purse and showing it to her. "This is more about what might come with mixing business with pleasure. I think I might be pregnant."

Stacy's eyes widen, and she scoots closer. "Oh, Allie. Have you taken the test yet?"

"No, I just picked it up after my shift," I tell her, feeling the weight of the situation settling between us.

"Well, I'm here, okay? Whatever you need," she says, her voice firm with unwavering support.

I nod, feeling a surge of gratitude for having her by my side. "Thanks. I think I just need to do this and find out for sure. I'm probably worrying over nothing, right?"

Stacy gives my hand a reassuring squeeze. "Right. But no matter what, I've got your back. Let's find out and deal with it from there."

I examine the box, my eyes scanning over the directions.

"It says it only takes a few minutes," I say with a weak smile.

With that, I hurry to the bathroom and do the deed. As soon as the test is done, I practically sprint back to my room. Just in the nick of time, too, as I hear our roommates' voices start to fill the apartment. Privacy is rare in our bustling shared space.

Stacy taps lightly on my door before entering and then closes it with a soft click, eyebrows raised in silent question. "Are you sure you did everything right?" she whispers.

"Yep, peed on a stick like a champ," I quip, trying to keep the mood light despite the butterflies doing somersaults in my stomach. "I mean, I'm on the pill, Stace. This should be a no-brainer, right?"

She nods, sitting down beside me on the bed. "How late are we talking here?" she asks, her tone gentle.

I throw my hands up, a little exasperated with myself. "At least a week ... maybe a bit more. My life's been a bit of a blur lately with the new job and sneaking around with the boss."

Stacy hums thoughtfully. "Any chance you've been sick? Sometimes, that can throw your cycle out of whack."

I shake my head, sinking back against the headboard. "Nope, no sniffles or anything. Just lots of forgetfulness apparently, and not thinking about schedules."

Our eyes are glued to my phone as the timer ticks down. It finally beeps, and we both jump a little. "Moment of truth,"

I announce, my heart thumping wildly as I reach for the stick.

We lean in close together, and I pull out the test. The little screen is merciless in its clarity.

Positive.

Well, shit.

CHAPTER 20

PATRICK

"Two risottos, one salmon, on the fly!" I call out, my voice sharp over the clatter of pans and the sizzle of oil.

The Tuesday evening rush at Savor is in full throttle, and I'm right in the thick of it, orchestrating the kitchen like a conductor. My gaze sweeps over the line cooks, ensuring precision and perfection on every plate.

Allie is at the grill tonight, her movements confident and skilled as she perfectly sears salmon, the skin crackling under the intense heat. Despite the rush, my eyes are drawn to her more often than not—not just because of what's going on between us but because I expect the best from her, just like I do from everyone else.

"Allie, I need that salmon yesterday!"

"Coming right up, Chef!" she responds with confidence. The scent of sizzling garlic and the sharp tang of freshly chopped herbs fill the air. The kitchen staff moves with a practiced choreography, each member adeptly handling their part, all under the cadence I set.

As I glance around, I notice something seems subtly off with Allie, even though she's performing flawlessly, her plating meticulous as she lays out grilled asparagus beside a perfectly cooked salmon.

Yet there's a withdrawn quality about her, a slight distance in her focus.

When a brief lull in the orders allows, I step closer to her station. "Allie, everything okay? You're on point with the orders, but you seem ... off," I say quietly, shielding our conversation from the rest of the kitchens' ears.

She looks up, her eyes meeting mine briefly. There's a flicker of something, hesitation, or maybe concern, before she masks it with a quick, practiced smile.

"Yeah, just focusing on not burning the place down with these sears," she jokes, a lightness to her tone.

I'm not entirely convinced but I nod anyway, respecting her professionalism and her space. "If there's anything you need to talk about ..." I let the offer hang, hoping she understands it's sincere.

She acknowledges it with a nod, her attention already back on her station. "Thanks, Chef. I'll keep the fires to the grill," she assures me.

As the pace picks back up, I retreat slightly, allowing her the room to work, but my thoughts remain on what could be troubling her. Something's up, and while the kitchen demands my full attention, I can't help but stay alert to any signs that Allie might need more than just a passing check-in.

As things begin to slow down, an idea forms. Caleb will be going away for a few days, and it seems like an opportune moment to invite her over. Her earlier distance had me concerned, but hearing her laughter echoing lightly across the kitchen gives me some reassurance. Maybe whatever was bothering her has resolved itself.

Just as I decide to approach her, Marissa, our hostess, intercepts me. Her expression is apologetic yet urgent.

"Chef, there are some guests out front requesting to see you. They insisted on waiting to speak with you directly," she reports.

I frown, instantly alert. "Were they a problem for you?" I ask, protective of my staff. It's essential that respect is maintained, no matter the circumstance.

"No, Chef, they weren't rude, just very insistent," Marissa clarifies quickly, sensing my concern.

Acknowledging her with a nod, I feel a sense of caution. "Thanks, Marissa. I'll handle it."

I head out of the kitchen, ready to confront whatever this unexpected issue might be, my mind half on Allie and the evening I hope we might still share.

As I enter the dining area, I realize, with a heavy sigh, that the restaurant is winding down for the night. Chairs are up on tables, and the floors are being vacuumed, but there's still one table occupied.

As I approach, I see Luca Amato sitting with a younger man who's the spitting image of him. A bottle of fine wine and three filled glasses are set up on their table, looking almost out of place in the quiet, mostly empty space.

The waiter, busy prepping for the next day, catches my eye and rushes over. "They insisted on the bottle after dinner, offered fifty over the asking price," he explains, a touch apologetic.

I chuckle, clapping him on the shoulder. "It's all good," I say, dismissing any concern with a wave of my hand as I continue toward the table.

Luca spots me coming and greets me with a nod, a slight smirk playing on his lips. "Patrick, come, sit," he gestures to the empty chair beside the other man. "This is my son, Donnie."

We shake hands, and the firm grip of the younger Amato tells me he's been well-schooled in the art of first impressions. I pick up the third glass, raising it slightly. "Thanks for the wine," I say, acknowledging the gesture.

Luca wastes no time, getting straight to the point as I settle into my seat. "Patrick, let's talk business. Do you have a price for our Tuesday evenings yet?" His tone is direct.

I nod, leaning forward slightly, my own tone businesslike but respectful. "I've crunched the numbers based on our average Tuesdays over the last year. For closing down the entire restaurant to accommodate your gatherings, here's the figure we're looking at."

I take out the small notepad and pen that I keep in my front coat pocket, jotting down a number and folding the piece of paper in half before handing it over.

Luca picks it up, eyeing the number with a seasoned gaze, then sets it down with a nod. "Fair enough, Patrick. But let's address any concerns you might have. Out in the open, yes?" he suggests, a faint smile playing on his lips.

I appreciate his straightforward approach. "Luca," I start, honoring his preference for informality, "my main concern is about the nature of these meetings. I run a tight ship here, and I need to ensure that whatever business you conduct won't bring any trouble to Savor's doorstep."

Luca chuckles at this, seeming to respect the directness. "I like you, Patrick. You're a straight shooter. Listen, we're just having dinner, talking shop. Nothing that will spill over and disrupt your business."

However, Donnie, who had been quietly observing until now, leans in, his expression tight. "Seems like you're looking for guarantees we can't give," he interjects, his voice sharp. "Are you looking to back out? Because we can definitely make it worth your while, or we can just as easily find another place that won't ask so many questions."

The air thickens with tension, and I hold Donnie's gaze unflinchingly. "I'm in the business of running a top-notch restaurant. Your money's good, but not if it costs me my reputation or brings the wrong kind of attention here. I'm sure you can understand that," I reply, my voice steady and definitive.

Luca raises his hand, gesturing for calm. "Donnie, let's keep it friendly. It's Patrick's right to ask these questions. He's protecting his interests, same as we would." Turning back to me, Luca smiles thinly. "You'll have no problems from us, Patrick. We're here to enjoy your food and your hospitality. That's all."

Luca, still holding his wine glass with an air of casual authority, slides a list across the table toward me after noting my agreement to a trial run. "We'll pay your price plus ten percent," he declares confidently, a clear sign of his intent to ensure his deal is appealing. "And you have my word, Patrick, there'll be no trouble from us."

I glance down at the list he's provided. It details the number of guests and the requirement for three servers and specifies that I personally oversee the menu for the evening. It's clear they're looking for an exclusive, tailored, and discreet experience.

"Just make sure the evening is memorable, Patrick," Luca adds, his tone indicating not just a request but an expectation.

As I'm about to respond, affirming that I can indeed craft a menu that will impress even the most discerning palates, the kitchen door suddenly swings open. Allie steps out, her presence like a sudden breeze that shifts the energy in the room.

CHAPTER 21

ALLIE

"Oops, sorry for the interruption," I quip as I halt mid-step, realizing I've just barged into what looks like a high-stakes meeting.

The two men with Patrick, oozing a vibe that's part *GQ* and part *Godfather*, give me a quick once-over.

Patrick, ever the cool captain of his ship, stands up smoothly. "No worries, Allie. Why don't you join us for a moment?" His invitation is all the reassurance I need to stride over, even though I feel wildly underdressed in my chef's gear. "Gentlemen, this is my newest sous chef, Allie Tucker."

As I approach, the older gentleman, introduced as Luca, stands up. Chivalry isn't dead, it seems, or maybe it's just good manners for show. "Ms. Tucker, a pleasure to meet you," he says, his voice smooth as aged whiskey, though his eyes are calculating.

Next, I'm introduced to Luca's son, Donnie. He's another story altogether. When we shake hands, he holds on a tad too long, his eyes doing a not-so-subtle up-and-down glance over my body that stops noticeably south of my face. I extract my hand with a swift tug, plastering on a smile that's more a bared-teeth warning than a friendly greeting.

Patrick jumps in like a pro, smoothing over the awkward edges. "Allie here is one of our top chefs at Savor," he tells them, his pride in my work clear in his voice.

Luca perks up. "Then we must owe much of tonight's exceptional dinner to Ms. Tucker?" His tone is appreciative but curt, as if he's used to getting more than just good food out of his conversations.

"That's right," Patrick confirms, giving me a quick, supportive look that says he's in my corner, no matter what high-rolling guests we have.

Donnie, meanwhile, has gone quiet, but his gaze is still stuck on me like some kind of unwelcome sauce. I decide to keep the conversation strictly culinary.

"I hope everything was to your satisfaction," I say, aiming for cheerful professionalism.

"Absolutely delightful, thank you," Luca responds; his smile widens just a bit as he settles back into his chair.

"Anyway, I figured we should all get acquainted since Allie will be assisting me next Tuesday," Patrick explains, his tone professional. "She'll be a key part of the evening's food."

Luca nods approvingly, his eyes assessing me but politely, while Donnie's eyes continue to linger a little too long, making my skin crawl. Patrick goes on to mention the names of the waitstaff that will be present, outlining the plan with the precision of a general.

As agreements are made and hands are shaken, Luca takes Patrick aside for a moment to go over one more detail. That's when the air shifts. The moment Luca is out of earshot, Donnie leans in, his voice dropping to a murmur that's meant to be charming but just comes off as sleazy.

"You know, you really shouldn't hide such a pretty face back in the kitchen all night," Donnie says, his breath giving off a whiff of wine. He winks as if we're sharing some private joke instead of him making an utterly inappropriate comment.

I stiffen, my smile fixed but my eyes cold. "I think I serve the guests best from the kitchen," I retort, my tone light but edged with steel. "That's where the magic happens, after all."

Patrick, catching the tail end of the exchange, frowns slightly, his gaze flicking between us.

"Allie is excellent at her job," he adds; there's a subtle undercurrent of warning in his voice that suggests he's not blind to Donnie's behavior.

Donnie laughs, a hollow sound that feels forced. "Just a suggestion," he says, leaning back in his chair, the picture of nonchalance. "It's always nice to see beautiful talent showcased, isn't it?"

I resist the urge to roll my eyes, instead turning to Patrick with a look that I hope communicates my irritation without words. Patrick nods slightly, an unspoken understanding passing between us.

Luca returns then, his timing impeccable, and the atmosphere shifts back to business. Handshakes are exchanged once more, this time signaling the end of the meeting. As the men prepare to leave, I step back, allowing Patrick to escort them out, my relief palpable.

I make a beeline back to the sanctuary of the kitchen. The taste of Donnie's sleazy comments still lingers unpleasantly, like garlic on the breath. He was absolutely scummy, and his leering was gross. It left me feeling uneasy and with a creeping sense of dread.

As I enter, the kitchen feels empty and unusually quiet. The bustling energy from earlier has dissipated. I start chopping onions for tomorrow's prep, but really, I'm just trying to banish the discomfort I feel from that meeting.

Moments later, Patrick storms back in, his face set in a hard line that I know all too well means trouble. He's definitely not happy, and something tells me it's not about the food cost or a missed delivery.

"What's up?" I ask, setting down my knife. "You look like you just smelled rotten eggs."

He sighs, pinching the bridge of his nose. "I didn't like how Donnie was looking at you. It was out of line," he states, his voice low and tense.

"Yeah, he gave me the creeps. I didn't like it one bit either," I reply, glad that we're on the same page but still feeling creeped out by the encounter.

Patrick's frown deepens, and he suggests, "Maybe we should use one of the other sous chefs next Tuesday. I don't want that guy anywhere near you."

I shake my head, not willing to let Donnie's sleaziness sideline me. "No. It'll be fun to run the show, just the two of us,"

I insist with a forced cheerfulness, trying to lighten the mood. "After all, we don't need the whole cavalry for just a handful of VIPs. We can handle it, and I'm not about to let that jerk scare me off."

Patrick studies me for a long moment, his eyes searching. Finally, he nods, albeit reluctantly. "All right. We'll do it together then," he agrees, a smile finally breaking through the anger. "But I'm keeping an eye on things. No one messes with my team."

Grateful for his support but determined not to let this shake me, I pick up my knife again, a renewed vigor in my slicing. "Let's show them how we do it at Savor. Nothing and no one is going to spoil our evening."

Patrick chuckles, the tension easing between us. "That's the spirit," he says.

Patrick looks contemplative, which means he's turning things over in his mind, planning out strategies like he's about to revamp the entire menu. Seeing him this way, I can't help but close the distance between us. I wrap my arms around his waist from behind, leaning my head against his back.

"Hey," I murmur, my voice muffled slightly by his chef's jacket. "You don't need to worry about a guy like Donnie. He couldn't catch my interest if he were the last man on earth with a recipe for eternal youth."

He turns in my embrace, his hands finding my shoulders as he looks down into my eyes. There's a softness there that makes my heart race just a bit faster. Then, without a word, he bends down and kisses me—a sweet, affirming kiss that speaks volumes.

But the kiss is short-lived as he pulls away, his eyes searching mine, serious yet full of something more tender. "Would you like to stay with me for the next few days? Caleb's out of town," he says, his voice hopeful.

The offer hangs in the air, tempting and full of possibilities. Part of me lights up at the thought of waking up next to him without sneaking around, of not having to say goodnight at the door. But I can't help but think of Caleb. This thing between Patrick and me is deepening, moving past the casual into something neither of us can ignore much longer. The question of telling Caleb about us looms large. And I still haven't found the right time and place to tell Patrick I'm pregnant.

I meet his gaze, seeing the same desire mirrored in his eyes that's swirling inside me. "I'd like that," I say, my voice steady despite the butterflies dancing in my stomach.

CHAPTER 22

ALLIE

As Patrick's front door swings open, it's like crossing into a different universe. Even though I've seen the house before, it still impresses me.

I can't help but let out a low whistle this time, feeling more confident and comfortable in our relationship.

"I have to ask how a chef can afford a palace like this. Savor must be printing money," I tease, trying to make light of the stark contrast between his place and my cramped apartment.

As soon as the words leave my mouth, a flush of embarrassment heats my cheeks.

Smooth, Allie, real smooth.

But Patrick just chuckles, shaking his head as he takes my coat. "The restaurant does okay, but Savor isn't my only gig. I've got a few investments here and there that do pretty well," he explains, leading me into the spacious living room that overlooks a manicured backyard.

My curiosity piqued, I can't help but wonder just how many zeroes are in his bank balance. But as he pulls a bottle of wine from a sleek, built-in rack, all thoughts of his finances start to fade away.

"I hope you like Pinot Noir," he says, effortlessly popping the cork. It should go well with the evening I have planned."

"Oh, no, I'm okay with just some water," I say, garnering a puzzled look from Patrick. Thankfully, he pulls a bottle of Perrier out instead of questioning my refusal of alcohol.

The smooth sound of jazz starts to fill the room as he hands me the water, soft saxophone riffs mingling with the clink of our glasses. I take a sip, the bubbles of the sparkling drink perfectly matching the sultry undercurrents of the music.

"You know, this is already dangerously close to perfect," I admit, feeling the warmth of the ambiance he's created starting to seep into my bones.

He smiles, that charming, confident grin that's all Patrick. "Only close? I'll have to try a bit harder then," he replies, his tone playful yet promising.

As we move to sit on the plush sofa, he raises his glass toward me. "To an evening of no interruptions and getting to know each other a little better."

I clink my glass against his, the spark in his eyes mirroring my own feelings. "To a very private tasting menu," I quip back, feeling bold under his gaze.

He laughs, a sound that stirs something deep inside me. "Oh, I assure you, the night's specials are definitely worth exploring."

I shoot Patrick a playful smirk. "So, what's on the menu for tonight?" I tease, giving my glass a little twirl as I sink deeper into the plush sofa cushions.

Patrick nods as he sips his wine, his expression shifting just a tad toward serious, but those twinkling eyes of his don't lose their shine. "I have a few ideas if you're up for it," he says, his voice dropping to a deliciously tempting pitch that makes my heart do a little skip.

I nod, and he continues.

"Tonight, I was thinking we could explore some boundaries, like you asked," he begins, his voice low and enticing. "Have you ever experimented with silk ropes or blindfolds, Allie?"

I shake my head, my curiosity clearly written across my face.

He smiles, picking up on my intrigue. "Imagine this," he continues, "silk ropes are gentle; they're about feeling the restraint without it hurting. It's more about the sensation of being held, of surrendering control in a way that's completely safe." He pauses, making sure I'm with him so far. I nod, completely drawn into the visualization.

"And then there's the blindfold," he adds, his eyes locking onto mine with a look that's both challenging and reassuring. "It heightens every other sense. When you're unable to see, every touch, every taste, every whisper becomes more intense, more electrifying."

He reaches over to the back of the sofa, pulling up a smooth, black silk blindfold and a length of matching silk rope. "When you allow me to place these on you," he continues, handling them with a familiarity that sends another wave of excitement through me, "you're trusting me to lead, to take care of you. It's all about enhancing the experience, pushing the boundaries just a little, in a way that we both enjoy."

I find myself nodding, the idea more appealing by the second. "It's all consensual," he stresses. "We'll go only as far as you're comfortable. We can stop at any time; you just need to say the word.

"Everything's built on trust, Allie. Nothing happens without your green light," he reassures me, his tone earnest and his gaze steady.

Feeling wrapped in the safety of his words, I nod, excitement mingling with a flutter of nerves. "I trust you, Patrick. I want to do this," I say, my voice bold and a bit daring.

His smile softens, radiating warmth as he reaches out to caress my cheek gently. "We'll take it slow, and remember, you can call it off anytime," he tells me, infusing the moment with tenderness.

It's not just his swanky house or the sultry jazz that makes me feel at ease—it's the protective atmosphere he's crafted with his respect for boundaries. "Show me these specials of yours," I reply in a sultry tone.

He stands and offers his hand, which I eagerly take, feeling the reassuring strength in his grip. He then leads me toward a more private area of his house, where we can explore without interruption.

I can't wait.

CHAPTER 23

ALLIE

The bedroom air crackles with electric anticipation as Patrick guides me in, a playful gleam in his eye. The soft evening light filters through the blinds, casting stripes across his strong forearms as he rolls up his sleeves. I perch on the edge of the bed, my heart racing with raw attraction.

"So, tell me, Allie," he starts, his voice low and enticing, vibrating straight through to my core. "What's your pleasure tonight? How far do you want to go exploring?"

I chew on my lip, thinking, then flash him a daring smile. "I think I'd like to try being tied up," I say, the words sending a thrilling shiver down my spine. His grin widens, delight and desire mingling in his expression.

"Perfect," he replies. "But first, how about you slip into something a bit more comfortable?"

I stand, feeling his intense gaze on me as I begin to slip out of my clothes. Patrick watches appreciatively, his approval clear as his eyes roam over my body, tracing my figure in a way that I love, with total lust in his eyes.

"Absolutely stunning," he says, and I can't help but preen a little under his gaze. It feels good to be adored like this.

He retrieves another length of soft, silk rope from the drawer—an intimate promise in his hands. This one is a fiery red, quite a stark contrast to the black one he showed me downstairs. "You trust me?" he asks.

"Completely," I assure him, my voice steady despite the butterflies dancing in my stomach. He walks around me and instructs me to put my hands behind my back, his fingers brushing lightly against my skin as he expertly ties the ropes. Each contact sends a jolt of anticipation through me.

Once he's finished, he locks eyes with me, his look intense. "You're beautiful like this," he says, reaching around and securing the final knot, "completely open to me, yet still so strong."

I test the bonds, finding them snug but not restrictive—perfect. "Your turn to show me what you've got," I tease, a playful challenge.

He steps back, meeting my challenge with a smirk. "Oh, I plan to, don't worry. But remember," he adds, leaning close, his breath tickling my ear, "we stop at your request. Anytime."

I nod, his serious tone reassuring me further. "I trust you," I whisper back.

Patrick's smile turns tender for a moment before he shifts into a more mischievous mode. "Now, let's see how much fun we can have."

He takes in a slow breath through his nose. "First. Get down on your knees."

It's awkward, but I'm able to do it. Soon, I'm on my knees in front of him, my legs tucked underneath me, my arms behind me. I grin as I stare at his erection, straining the fabric of his slacks.

"Don't tell me I have to take that out without my hands."

He grins. "I can help you out. But just a little."

Patrick undoes his belt and zipper, and I'm practically licking my lips in anticipation. Finally, he reaches into his boxer briefs and pulls out his cock, hard and dripping with precum, ready for me.

I don't need to be told what to do next. My instinct is to wrap my fingers around his length and stroke him to feel his hot, hard warmth. But I'm bound. Everything has to be done with my mouth.

I lean forward, flashing him a smile before kissing his head. The salty taste of the precum dances on my lips, encouraging me. I tease him a little before opening my mouth and taking his tip inside, wrapping my lips tightly around him.

God, he tastes so fucking good. I make a slow circle around his head with my tongue, and he groans with pleasure, gazing down at me with hungry eyes. When I'm ready to, I venture down further and further, taking as much of him into my mouth as I can.

I travel back up, then repeat, kissing and licking his tip each time I reach the top. It's so freaking sexy having him stand over me, his powerful body on full display as I bring him close to orgasm. It was a little weird at first not being able to use my hands, but the more I suck him, the hotter it is to think about making him explode with nothing more than my lips and my tongue.

I don't get the chance, however. Patrick reaches down and guides me over to the bed. When I'm near, he undoes the binding but holds my hands together, tying them to the headboard instead as I lay on my back.

He takes off his clothes, stripping down to nothing, his cock glistening from my work.

"You look so damn sexy like this, bound and ready for me. How do you feel?"

"Like I need you inside me right now."

He grins, climbing over top of me.

"Not just yet. Not until I taste you."

With that, he moves to the end of the bed, slipping his arms underneath me and guiding my legs over his shoulders, positioning himself perfectly to please me with his mouth.

He kisses my thighs and then my lips, the pleasure building and building by the second.

Finally, his tongue touches my clit, and I melt.

"Oh ... Oh yes ..."

He eats me with total relish, licking my clit and sucking my lips. His tongue occasionally moves from my clit, plunging inside of me, giving me just a whisper of a hint at how good his cock will feel.

His attention returns to my clit, and he's guiding me right to the cusp of orgasm. My back arches and I prepare to let go, prepare to give in. When the orgasm arrives, it's like a series of crashing waves that overwhelm me, making my whole body feel warm and alive.

As the climax begins to wane, Patrick wastes no time going back to work, tying my ankles to the bed. I'm totally bound now, still buzzing from my orgasm.

"Please," I said. "I can't take any more teasing. I need it."

He chuckles, and the devilish expression that plays on his handsome face suggests that teasing me is exactly what he has in mind.

But mercifully, he doesn't. Instead, he gets onto his knees in between my legs, positioning himself perfectly to glide into me.

"Do you want it?" he asks.

"I do. So, fucking badly."

"Then ask nicely."

I smile, hating but loving when he does this to me.

"Please. Please, Patrick."

With his eyes locked on mine, he pushes into me with a slow, deep thrust. I close my eyes and moan, focusing on the sensation of his cock driving into me, stretching me out and filling me completely. He places his hand on my belly, holding me in place as he buries himself to the root.

My breasts bounce up and down as he picks up his pace, bucking into me. I want to go wild, to grab onto his body, his ass, run my hands through his hair. But I can't, so all of my energy becomes focused on the pleasure, the sensation of his cock inside of me.

"Come for me," he says. "Right now."

There's no chance even to reply. The orgasm has been building so much that all I can do is nod as it releases. I clench around him, and Patrick comes with me, letting out an animalistic grunt as he erupts inside of me, filling me with his warmth.

Everything slows down, and the world is reduced to the two of us breathing in tandem as we recover. Finally, he undoes the knots, my limbs falling limply onto the bed. He moves next to me, wrapping his arm around me and pulling me flush against him.

He kisses my shoulder.

"How was that?"

"Wonderful."

We lay like that in silence for a long time, sleep drifting in. And as I doze off in his arms, I know I'm just where I want to be.

CHAPTER 24

PATRICK

"Let's kick off with the hors d'oeuvres," I begin. "Bacon-wrapped scallops, as requested by Luca. We'll add a touch of maple glaze for a sweet and smoky finish."

The kitchen is abuzz as Allie and I gear up for the exclusive dinner tonight. We've meticulously designed a five-course meal that's both modern and tantalizing and hopefully up to the snuff of Luca and his crew.

Allie deftly wraps each plump scallop with bacon, her hands steady and sure. "Hope they like this."

"They better. And let's keep the surprises coming," I reply, sharing a conspiratorial grin with her.

As we dive into the intricate dance of dinner preparation, Allie and I find ourselves working shoulder-to-shoulder, the proximity intensifying the electric charge between us. I'm trying to concentrate on the meticulous tasks at hand—perfecting the bacon-wrapped scallops and adjusting the aioli drizzle—yet I find myself repeatedly drawn to her. Her fragrance, a subtle mix of her shampoo and the faint scent of citrus fills my senses, distracting me in a way that no other woman has before.

I catch myself watching her a little too intently as she laughs softly while adjusting the appetizer. Our eyes meet, and the corner of her mouth twitches upwards in a playful smirk.

"Careful, Chef," she teases. "You might end up burning something."

I chuckle, shaking my head slightly to clear the distraction. "Just making sure everything is perfect," I reply, though we both know my focus had drifted from the food.

I lean in slightly, lowering my voice. "Speaking of perfect, I've been thinking about our last experiment," I say, the memory of our recent exploration into BDSM making her cheeks flush a delightful shade of pink.

Her eyes light up with mischief, and a playful grin spreads across her face. "Well, if tonight is a hit, we'll definitely need to celebrate," she suggests.

I match her grin, feeling a surge of anticipation. "You're on," I reply.

As Allie and I finish prepping the last of the hors d'oeuvres, my phone buzzes in my pocket. I pull it out to see a text from Luca.

We'll be there in 30 minutes.

I show Allie the message, and a spark of excitement flickers in her eyes.

"Showtime," I say. "Let's see how they like the new twists on the classics tonight."

Just then, the front-of-house team starts filtering in. I gather the hostess, a bartender, and the three servers around us in the kitchen.

"Listen up, everyone," I begin, all business now. "Tonight's a big one. We've got some high-profile guests coming in, and I want everything to run like clockwork. Each of you plays a key part in making tonight a success. If all goes well, you'll all share in tonight's bonus. Let's make sure we give them an experience they won't forget."

As I lay out the plans, Allie is by my side, her gaze fixed on me. I catch her biting her lip briefly, an action that's subtly seductive and wholly distracting. God, she's magnetic, even when she's just standing there.

"Let's keep our focus sharp tonight, okay?"

The chorus of "Yes, Chef!" is the response.

Allie smiles, a glint of mischief in her eyes. As the staff disperses to their stations, readying for the evening, I pull her aside for a quick word.

"Thanks for being right here with me," I say, quieter now. "Tonight's menu has pieces of both of us in it."

She nods, her expression serious but supportive. "Let's blow them away. With our food, our service—everything."

I step into the unusually quiet dining area of Savor, noting the silence where there's typically a bustling dinner crowd. It's a reminder of how far I've come—success is becoming our norm, and I can almost taste that Michelin Star on the horizon.

But my ambitions are momentarily put on hold as Luca Amato and his crew roll in—twelve sharp-dressed men looking like they own the place. The hostess hesitates under their imposing presence, so I quickly step in to take charge.

Striding over confidently, I shake Luca's hand with a firm grip. "Luca, great to see you again," I greet him with a warm nod. The group responds with nods and mumbled greetings, but my eyes are drawn to Donnie. He's scanning the room, clearly on the lookout for Allie, and it sets my teeth on edge.

I hide my irritation as I guide them to their table. "We've put together something special for you tonight," I tell Luca as I hand him the menu, briefly running through the dishes we've prepared. His eyes scan the offerings, a flicker of anticipation passing over his features. "Looking forward to your feedback," I add, with a slight challenge in my tone.

"Looking forward to this meal," Luca replies with a smile.

As they settle in, I make it clear, "If you need anything, just signal. We're here to make sure you have a top-notch experience tonight."

After ensuring they're comfortably seated, I pull the hostess and a couple of servers aside. "Keep a tight watch on them, especially Donnie. Let me know if he tries anything or starts snooping around," I instruct firmly, ensuring they understand the gravity without causing a scene.

Heading back to the kitchen, I'm all business.

I push through the swinging doors, finding Allie already deep in her preparations. Her focus momentarily breaks as she looks up, a flicker of concern crossing her features.

"Is Donnie here?" she asks, trying to sound nonchalant, but there's an edge to her voice.

"Yeah, he's out there," I confirm, keeping my tone steady. "Don't let him get to you, though. He's just some punk who thinks too highly of himself."

She exhales, forcing a smile that doesn't quite hide her unease. "I know, it's stupid. But there's something about him that's unsettling."

I nod, understanding her instincts. Guys like Donnie often have more than just arrogance backing them up; they might even have real danger in their past. But I keep these darker thoughts to myself; no need to add to her worries.

With the rest of the staff busy up front, it's just us in the kitchen, a rare moment of privacy. I step closer, pulling her gently by the waist. "Let me help take your mind off of him," I say and lean in to kiss her, slow and deep, pouring reassurance and passion into the gesture. "Tonight's going to be incredible," I murmur against her lips.

She melts into the kiss for a moment, then pulls back with a bright smile. "I agree. Let's make it a night to remember," she says, her earlier concerns momentarily forgotten.

We turn together to face the stoves and counters, our private world where we both shine. As she dives back into her culinary ballet, her skill and grace on full display, a thought strikes me with the weight of a well-aged wine—this isn't just admiration I feel for her. It's deeper, stronger.

Watching her move with such precision and passion, the realization dawns on me: I might just be in love.

CHAPTER 25

ALLIE

"I don't want to come off as arrogant," I say, setting my fork down with a clink, "but this might just be the best meal I've ever had a hand in."

Patrick and I are putting the final garnishes on the entrees, a masterpiece of culinary perfection just waiting to be savored. As the serving staff sweeps the plates away to our guests, we set aside one extra dish of the duck entree for ourselves—a chef's perk.

Together, we dive into the sample, a seamless blend of flavors that makes me close my eyes in appreciation. It's absolutely freaking divine.

Patrick grins, his eyes sparkling with pride and something tender that makes my stomach do a little flip. "It's one of my finest, too," he admits. "Couldn't have reached this level without you."

The decadent meal doesn't quite quell the thrill his words send through me. As the last of the entrees leave the kitchen, Patrick glances at the clock. "We've got a little time before we need to prep the desserts. You want to take a breather?"

Part of me—a rather bold part—wants to suggest we take that breather in his office, maybe lock the door for a bit. But I bite my tongue, keeping those thoughts firmly in check, at least for now.

"Sounds like a plan," I manage, trying to keep my tone light.

As I start to step away, Patrick's hand lands gently on my shoulder, stopping me in my tracks. His touch is warm, reassuring, and a little distracting. He looks me straight in the eyes, his gaze sincere. "Really, Allie, thank you. Tonight wouldn't be what it is without your hard work."

His gratitude warms me more than the bustling heat of the kitchen. "Hey, the night's not over yet," I remind him with a playful wag of my finger, trying to keep the mood light despite the fluttering in my chest.

He chuckles, a low sound that rumbles within. "You're right about that," he says in that husky tone that always seems to find its way right under my skin. "And I'm looking forward to every minute of it."

His words linger in the air between us, charged and promising. With a final glance, I head off to grab that breather, my mind racing not just with the success of our meal but with the tantalizing possibilities of what the rest of the evening might hold.

I make my way out of the kitchen, heading for the staff restroom, but then it hits me—the guests tonight are all men, no women. Why not indulge in a little luxury and use the posh patron restrooms upfront? If you can't join them, at least share their marble sinks, right?

Stepping onto the main dining floor, the scene strikes me like a raucous Italian dinner straight out of a movie. Glasses clink, laughter rumbles, and the rich aroma of food mingles with the deep notes of red wine in the air. It's vibrant, lively, almost theatrical.

As I navigate through the dining room, Luca spots me. He stands up, a respectful nod to old-school chivalry, and strides over with a wide, appreciative smile.

"Everyone, a moment, please," he announces, raising his voice over the chatter. The table quiets down a bit as all eyes turn to me. "Allie, this young lady here," he gestures to me with a flourish, "is the brains behind the incredible meal we're enjoying tonight."

I can feel my cheeks warm under the spotlight. "Oh, it's very much a team effort," I quickly deflect, nodding toward the kitchen where Patrick is masterminding the rest of the evening. "Couldn't have done it without the big man in the back."

Luca laughs, clapping me on the shoulder. "Modest, too! We like that," he says, which earns a round of approving nods and toasts from the table. I can't help but smile, grateful for the recognition but eager to escape the spotlight.

As I'm soaking in the praise, my gaze inadvertently meets Donnie's. His eyes are on me, intense and unsettling, like he's trying to peel back every layer with just his stare. It makes my skin crawl.

Thankfully, Luca, oblivious to the undercurrents, gives me a congenial nod. "Go on then; we won't keep you from your work. And we can't wait to see what comes out next!"

I murmur my thanks and make my escape, hurrying toward the sanctuary of the bathroom. The marble floors and gilded mirrors of the patron restroom offer a brief respite from the intensity of the dining room. Inside, I take a moment to breathe, leaning against the cool marble of the sink.

I straighten up, fixing a stray lock of hair, steeling myself for the rest of the evening. It's going to be a long night, and I need to be on top of my game—not just for the guests, but to handle whatever Donnie might throw my way.

My reflection seems to ask the tough questions I've been dodging all evening. The whole pregnancy is like a giant elephant in the room, and the idea of breaking the news to Patrick is just daunting. When's the right time to drop a bombshell like that? Surely not during a dinner rush over a plate of meticulously prepared hors d'oeuvres.

My mind races with possibilities, none of them particularly comforting. Patrick's a chef to his core, married to the kitchen. The scary thought that he might see this news as just another complication plays over and over in my mind, something he could maybe solve with a check and a pat on the back. But I've seen him with Caleb, and he's a great dad, engaging and caring. It gives me a sliver of hope.

Speaking of Caleb, how will he take the news that his ex is pregnant with his little brother or sister?

I splash some water on my face, trying to cool the flush of anxiety. I need to keep it together, at least until we get through tonight's dinner service. I'm psyching myself up to have that chat with Patrick soon, once the plates have cleared and we can maybe have a moment of peace.

Drying off my face, I straighten up, smoothing down my chef's jacket. No more moping around. The night's not over yet and the kitchen calls. Time to slap on my game face and get back to the pass. The personal stuff will have to wait just a bit longer.

I check myself out in the mirror one last time, take a deep breath, and head back to the heat of the kitchen, ready to tackle whatever the night throws my way.

As I'm about to push open the door and leave the bathroom, Donnie's unmistakable voice drifts in from just outside. He's chatting with one of his buddies, and they're deep in a conversation that's all too familiar, boasting and swapping crude stories about women.

Rolling my eyes, I grip the door handle tighter, ready to make a quick exit. But then it hits me—if I step out now, I'd be walking straight into them. No thanks. I'd rather not get tangled up in whatever sleazy tale they're spinning tonight.

Leaning back against the wall of the restroom, I tell myself it'll just be a minute more. They'll move along soon, I hope.

Just as I'm starting to tune them out, a snippet of their conversation catches my attention.

"—just need to take care of the guy," Donnie says.

Hearing that, I freeze in place, and my heart thumps a bit harder. Take care of the guy? That doesn't sound like they're planning a farewell party.

I inch closer to the door, my ear practically glued to the wood, trying to catch every word. My mind races through the possibilities—none of them good. Is this just macho posturing, or is there something more sinister at play?

As I strain to listen, the voices become clearer. They're discussing someone who seems to be a problem, someone who's in the way. The conversation dips into details, money involved, timing. My stomach tightens. This isn't just locker room talk; it sounds like they're plotting a murder.

"Yeah, you know the one; he's starting to be a real pain," Donnie's voice carries through the door, his tone dismissive but laced with annoyance. "I'm tired of waiting around for my big shot, you know? It's time for me to make a name for myself."

The other man, his voice lower, sounds hesitant. "Donnie, you know that's just asking for trouble. I don't even need to tell you all the shit that could go wrong. Are we ready for that?"

Donnie's laugh is shallow and humorless. "Maybe that's exactly what we need: a show of strength. I'm fed up with this bullshit, tired of always being treated like a fuckin' kid."

There's a pause, the kind that fills the air with tension before the other man sighs. "All right, if you think it's time, then it's time. But when this is all over and done, you'd better remember how I stuck my neck out for you."

"Don't worry," Donnie agrees, his voice firm. "You'll be right there with me at the top."

Their footsteps start to fade as they walk away, their voices dropping to a murmur before disappearing completely.

I'm left frozen against the wall, my mind racing. This wasn't just some tough-guy talk or business rivalry; they were discussing something far more dangerous. It's like something straight out of *The Sopranos*, except it's real, and it's happening right here in my workplace. They were talking about killing someone—an actual hit.

My hands shake slightly as the reality of what I've just overheard sets in. I need to tell Patrick, but where do I start? How do I explain that a potential murder is being plotted in his restaurant?

As I weave back through the kitchen, the gears in my head are grinding hard. Patrick's cozy monthly deal with the Amato crew, clearing out the restaurant for their private dinners, now seems way more dangerous than what I signed up for.

How could I have missed the obvious? Here I am, thinking I'm just whipping up five-star dishes, when it turns out I might be stirring the pot in a whole other world.

The idea of tangling with the mafia—even on the fringes—has me kicking myself. I've seen enough movies and read enough headlines to know that this isn't just some thrilling plot twist—it's a real danger. Walking away from the job might seem like a simple fix. Cut ties, turn in my apron, and just disappear into the night.

But then there's the not-so-little issue of the tiny human growing inside me. Quitting would not be merely walking away from my job; I'd also be walking away from Patrick, who happens to be the father of my baby. I'm more tied up in this mess than I realized.

Is Patrick just making a risky business move, or is there something darker lurking in those handshakes? The thought chills me. If he's mixed up in something dangerous, what does that mean for me? For our kid?

Once these kitchen doors close tonight, I'm going to need some real answers from Patrick. I have to know what kind of trouble we're really in.

CHAPTER 26

PATRICK

Back in the kitchen, I notice Allie slipping through the door, her usual spark dimmed. Something's off. I keep my voice even as I ask her, "Is everything okay?"

She offers me a weak smile. "Yeah, everything's fine." It doesn't take a genius to see she's far from fine, but I decide not to press her. Now's not the time.

"Let's focus on finishing up that dessert," I say instead, shifting our attention to the night's culinary finale.

The waitstaff buzzes in just then, ready for their next move. I quickly brief them, "Get espressos ready and see if our guests need anything before we serve dessert."

Once they scatter to attend to the guests, I find a moment to close the distance between Allie and me. Taking her hand gently, I raise it to my lips and kiss her knuckles, trying to bring some lightness back. "Can't wait to have you all to myself tonight," I murmur, hoping to see a genuine smile.

She smiles back, but it's forced, a shadow still lurking behind her gaze. "Me too," she says, but the enthusiasm isn't there.

Her reaction causes a knot in my stomach. Whatever's weighing on her, it's serious. I squeeze her hand, conveying silent support. Right now, I have to respect her space, but later, I need to find out what's really going on. We need to be open with each other, especially if we're going to make this work, not only in the kitchen but beyond it.

As the waitstaff takes the desserts out, I stand by the serving window, keeping an eye on the room as each dish lands on the tables. The reaction from Luca's table is immediate; even from my standpoint, I can tell they're impressed.

The evening stretches on, the clock ticking past the usual closing hours, but the atmosphere at the party remains buoyant, fueled by good food and better wine. The waitstaff hovers close by; their service has been impeccable, and as the night finally begins to wind down, their efforts are rewarded—each one grinning as they pocket hefty tips from the appreciative guests.

I step out of the kitchen to see the last of the men preparing to leave. Their praise is effusive as they thank me, some even pulling out wads of cash, offering me a little something extra. I hold up a hand, stopping them with a friendly but firm shake of my head.

"Thank you, but Mr. Amato has already taken care of everything," I tell them.

I walk them to the door, the cool night air a welcome relief after the heat of the kitchen. "We'll see you all next month," I say.

Luca extends his hand with a warm smile. "Thank you, Patrick, for an outstanding evening. My assistant will be in touch with you later this week to iron out the details for our next meeting."

I grasp his hand firmly, matching his smile with my own. "It was my pleasure, Luca. We look forward to having you back."

As the last of the guests filter out, Donnie lingers behind, swaggering over with a grin that's too arrogant to be friendly. His speech is slightly slurred, the alcohol loosening his tongue more than usual. He leans in a bit too close, his breath heavy with the scent of expensive wine.

"Hey, Patrick, that sexy blonde chef of yours," he starts, his voice a low drawl, "she's something else. I'd like to get to know her better."

I feel my jaw tighten, the muscles in my neck tensing up. On the surface, I keep my expression smooth, offering him a polite smile. "Actually, she and I are together," I reply, my tone even but firm, hoping to cut this line of conversation short.

Donnie bursts into laughter, a loud, obnoxious sound that echoes slightly in the empty dining room. He claps me on the back with a bit too much force. "Good for you, man! But hey," he adds with a wink, "if things ever go south, you let me know. I'd take a shot at that."

I stiffen under the weight of Donnie's hand on my back, his laughter grating on my nerves. As he insinuates his interest in Allie, my patience snaps.

"Watch it, kid," I say sharply, my tone low and firm, leaving no room for misinterpretation. "You will respect her when you're talking to me. She's not up for discussion or for grabs."

Donnie pauses, his smile faltering as he meets my glare. He straightens up, the cockiness in his posture receding slightly. "All right," he says with a dismissive wave, but his eyes harden. "Just saying, a guy like me? I don't need to wait for permission. I can have my pick of the city, taken or not."

His words hang in the air, a veiled threat wrapped in a smirk. I hold his gaze, unyielding. "Let's keep it professional, Donnie. That's best for everyone."

"Careful, Chef," he says. "Talking like that to a man like me is an easy way to end up pureed."

I want to strangle the little prick on the spot, but one of us is going to have to be the bigger man if I don't want this night to end in a fistfight with a Mafia boss's son.

"Good night, Donnie."

He finally heads out, leaving a trail of chuckles behind him. I lock the door with more force than necessary, the click of the deadbolt sounding overly loud in the quiet restaurant.

Alone, I lean against the door, taking a moment to gather myself. Disgust curdles in my stomach—not just at Donnie's words but at the reminder of the type of individuals my business now entertains. The decision comes easily; it's one I should have made earlier.

Shaking my head, I make my way back to the kitchen to oversee the final cleanup.

As I step through the doors, I notice Allie already elbow-deep in the post-service cleanup. There's a focus in her movements, a determination that's palpable even from across the room.

"Hey," I call out, crossing the kitchen to stand beside her. "You were amazing tonight, you know that?"

She glances up at me, a small smile tugging at the corners of her lips. "Thanks, Chef," she replies, her voice carrying a hint of weariness. "It was a pleasure working with you, as always."

I feel a pang of disappointment at her subdued response. Normally, this would be the time for banter, for playful flirtation to cap off a successful evening. But tonight, the air between us feels heavy with unspoken tension.

I open my mouth to say something more, to inject a bit of levity into the moment, but a glance at Allie's expression gives me pause. There's a distance in her eyes, a barrier that tells me now's not the time for idle chatter.

Instead, I nod in understanding, giving her a gentle squeeze on the shoulder before turning to join her in the cleanup. As we work side by side, the clatter of dishes and the swish of water filling the silence, I can't shake the nagging feeling that something's bothering her.

We should be celebrating tonight's success, reveling in the buzz of a job well done, but Allie's demeanor tells me otherwise.

I steal glances at her whenever I can, trying to decipher the thoughts swirling behind those expressive eyes. But she remains guarded, her focus locked on the task at hand.

As we wrap up the cleanup, Allie breaks the silence. "You know, you're right on the verge of getting that star," she says casually.

I pause, my hands still. "Star?" I ask, even though I know exactly what she's hinting at.

She flashes a knowing smile over her shoulder. "Michelin," she clarifies, her tone playful yet serious. "It's pretty rare for a new place like Savor to be in the running for a Michelin Star so quickly, but then, Savor isn't exactly commonplace, is it?"

Her words strike a chord. Moved by her confidence in me, I close the distance between us.

"I don't want it to be just me earning that star, Allie," I tell her firmly, taking her hand to stop her diligent scrubbing. "I want it to be *us*. We're in this together."

The warmth in her smile tells me she gets it. We're a team, in and out of the kitchen. I lean in and kiss her, sealing our shared commitment and dreams.

With the kitchen finally spotless and our work done, we walk out together.

We drive back to my place in quiet comfort, still riding the high from tonight's success. Once inside, I head to the fridge to grab a bottle of champagne, eager to keep the celebratory vibe going. "How about something to celebrate?" I ask, reaching for the glasses.

Her reaction is quick. "Actually, I'd rather not have alcohol tonight," she says, her voice a bit hesitant.

I nod and switch gears. "Sparkling cider, then?" I suggest, and she agrees more warmly this time. I pour us each a glass, and we toast to the future—ours and Savor's.

We sip the cider in silence before I lean in for a kiss, caught up in the moment. She pulls back sooner than expected, an apologetic smile on her face. "I might not be up for much tonight; I'm pretty tired," she admits.

I sense there's more she's not saying, but I let it be. Instead, I suggest, "Let's just relax then," and she seems relieved.

We head to bed, and she curls up next to me. I wrap my arms around her, comforted by her presence. Even though she's holding something back, I'm content just to have her here. Holding her close, I think about the future that awaits us.

As sleep edges in, I find myself smiling.

CHAPTER 27

ALLIE

I wake up alone in bed, but the delicious smells wafting in from the kitchen tell me Patrick's up to something good. I stretch and can't help but feel a twinge of guilt for being so distant last night. It wasn't fair to him, especially after such a big night at Savor, but between the pregnancy and what I overheard in the bathroom last night, my mind's still swirling.

I grab my phone and see a barrage of texts from Stacy, each more dramatic than the last:

Good morning! Did you spill the tea yet?

You can't just leave me in suspense! What'd he say?

Helloooo, are you ignoring me? I'm literally on the edge of my seat here!

I chuckle, feeling her impatience vibrating through the phone. I type a quick reply to calm her down, or at least try to.

But then my thoughts drift back to Donnie from last night, his creepy stares and that sleazy grin. Just the memory of them makes my skin crawl. How am I supposed to concentrate on work with that murder plot lurking in the background?

Shaking off the ick, I decide it's time to face the music—and the yummy smells. Maybe a good breakfast will give me the boost I need to finally tell Patrick about the baby.

With a deep breath and a plan to tackle one thing at a time, I toss the covers back and head to the closet. Time to turn on the charm and ease into the big news.

I quickly throw on one of Patrick's dress shirts, taking a moment to savor the scent that lingers on the fabric, and step out of the bedroom.

Pausing at the doorway of a spare bedroom, I'm struck by how unused it seems, like a blank canvas waiting for a new picture. The morning sunlight streams through the window, bathing the room in a warm, inviting glow. I step inside, my eyes imagining where a crib could go and picturing cheerful kids' decor brightening up the walls and a soft carpet strewn with toys. It's so easy to envision a child's laughter filling up this space.

The daydream snaps me back to reality with a pang of urgency. I need to talk to Patrick, and I need to do it today. With a deep breath, I turn from the potential nursery and head toward the kitchen, the aroma of breakfast growing stronger.

Patrick stands at the stove, expertly maneuvering a slotted spoon to retrieve perfectly poached eggs from a simmering pot. One glance at the setup, and I recognize the makings of eggs Benedict. My stomach growls in anticipation.

"Morning," I call out, trying to keep my voice light despite the butterflies fluttering in my stomach about the conversation ahead.

Patrick glances over his shoulder, his smile bright and welcoming. "Good morning," he replies cheerfully. "I see you've raided my wardrobe," he adds, his eyes flicking appreciatively down to the dress shirt I've thrown on. It hangs loosely on me, barely covering my thighs.

I laugh, a blush creeping up my cheeks. "I like your style," I tease back, admiring his relaxed morning look. He's wearing a sleeveless shirt that shows off his toned arms and lounge pants that hug his form exactly right, especially around his butt. I can't help but let my gaze linger a little longer than necessary.

"Hope you're hungry," he says, turning back to his task but still wearing that easy, inviting smile. He plates the eggs with a practiced hand, layering them over toasted English muffins and a generous helping of hollandaise sauce. The dish looks like something out of a gourmet magazine.

As he sets the plates on the kitchen island, I pull up a stool, still a bit distracted by the swirl of thoughts regarding our future and how to broach the topic of the pregnancy.

Patrick notices as I push the food around my plate, lost in thought. He puts his fork down and reaches across the table, taking my hand gently. His touch is warm and grounding.

"Whatever's on your mind, we can talk about it," he says, his voice calm and reassuring. "We're in this together, remember? We can work through anything."

His words, so full of trust and partnership, make my heart swell even as they collide with the anxiety of my thoughts. I look into his eyes, finding the strength I need in his steady gaze.

"I'm pregnant," I say softly, watching every shift in his expression, every minute reaction.

For a moment, Patrick just stares, his face unreadable. Then, a mix of emotions plays across his features—surprise, confusion, perhaps a flicker of fear. He leans back slightly, his voice carrying a note of disbelief.

"You're *what?*"

"Pregnant."

He stares off into space for a moment but quickly composes himself. It's the most out of sorts I've ever seen him.

"I thought I was done with diapers and midnight feedings," he mumbles, his tone bordering on incredulous.

I don't like his words. They sound like a dismissal, a step back from the responsibility looming ahead.

His reaction stings more than I expected. I feel a sharp pang of hurt, and without thinking, I pull my hand back from his grasp. "If you're not interested in being a part of this, I can handle it on my own," I say, my voice firm, even though my heart is racing. I'm not going to force him to be in the baby's life, but the hurt is hard to mask.

His expression shifts from surprise to concern as he realizes the impact of his words. "No, Allie, that's not what I meant," he starts, his tone changing as he reaches for my hand again, trying to bridge the gap he's inadvertently created.

"That's what you felt. It was your first reaction."

Before Patrick can say another word, I'm already up from the table and striding toward the bedroom with purpose. My chair squeaks a dramatic farewell as I march away to pack up my things.

I'm busy stuffing belongings into my bag when I hear Patrick's hastening footsteps.

"I'll just grab a cab," I announce, zipping up my bag with more force than necessary. The room fills with a tense silence that hangs heavy between us. "No reason for me to be here if you don't want me to be."

He closes the distance quickly, his hand catching my arm gently.

"Allie, wait," he pleads, drawing me into a firm hug before I can protest. His embrace envelops me, warm and reassuring, and I reluctantly melt a little despite myself. "I'm sorry for how I reacted," he murmurs, his voice muffled in my hair. "I didn't mean to come across as uncaring; I was just caught off guard."

He steps back just enough to look at me, his hands shifting to rest lightly on my stomach. The serious look in his eyes softens into something tender and warm. "I'd be honored to raise a child with a woman as amazing as you," he says.

"You mean that?"

He smiles. "How the hell could I not?"

The ice around my heart thaws instantly. I peer up at him, searching for any trace of doubt, but all I see is genuine affection and a hint of awe.

"Thank you, Patrick," I whisper, my earlier resolve softening into a smile.

Maybe we'll be in this together after all.

CHAPTER 28

ALLIE

"You know," I start, tossing a playful glance over my shoulder, "for a guy who's a wizard in the kitchen, you sure have a knack for turning up the heat without any appliances."

The morning unfolds with a lighthearted ease, sunlight bathing the space in a warm golden hue. As we move toward the bed, the rays spill across the floor, enhancing the intimate, cozy vibe of Patrick's well-kept sanctuary.

Patrick's laugh is a low rumble, soothing yet thrilling. "Believe me, I've got a few secret recipes," he says, his voice a soft growl as he steps towards me. "The key ingredient? Anticipation."

Matching his approach, I close the distance between us, my bare feet silent on the cool wood floor.

"Anticipation, huh?" I tease, reaching out to lightly tug at the hem of his shirt. "That sounds delicious. What else are you mixing up for us?"

He captures my hand and pulls it to his lips, kissing my fingertips gently. "Let's just say I plan to keep things interesting," he whispers, sending tingles up my arm.

"Show me," I challenge, with a flirtatious raise of my eyebrows.

Our banter fades as our lips meet, the kiss deepening with a passionate urgency that's been simmering since last night. Patrick's hands are warm as they slide to the small of my back, his touch firm yet tender, pulling me flush against him. The feel of his body, strong and sure, envelops me in a sense of complete safety and excitement.

Pulling back slightly, he looks into my eyes, intensity flickering in his gaze. "Ready to explore some more?" he asks, his voice husky.

"Absolutely," I breathe out, my pulse quickening as his fingers find the buttons of the shirt that I'm wearing.

With careful movements, he undoes each button, his fingertips grazing my skin, leaving a hot trail that only heightens my anticipation. The shirt falls open, and he peels it away, his eyes appreciating the view before him.

"You're breathtaking," he murmurs genuinely, his admiration making me blush.

I giggle softly, feeling bold and utterly charmed. "Your turn," I say, reaching for the hem of his shirt, pulling it up and over his head in one smooth motion. As I expose his chest, my fingers can't help but trace the contours of his muscles, appreciating the feel of him under my touch.

I take his hand, my heart dancing with delight as he leads me to the bed. The silk ropes and blindfold from before still lie there. As he ties the first gentle knot, a thrill courses through me.

"Remember," he says softly as he adjusts the blindfold, ensuring my comfort, "this is all about trust. You set the pace."

I nod, feeling a surge of affection and excitement. "I trust you completely," I reaffirm, letting the darkness of the blindfold heighten my other senses.

The room falls into a hushed silence, broken only by our shared breaths, as Patrick carefully ties the silk rope around my wrists.

Despite the blindfold obscuring my vision, I feel more attuned to every touch, every shift in the air. The silk is smooth and cool against my skin, and I wait with bated breath for what will come next. "Is that okay?" Patrick's voice is low and close to my ear, his breath warming my cheek.

"Perfect," I assure him, my voice a whisper of excitement. The sensation of being gently bound, combined with my inability to see, sharpens my other senses to an exquisite degree. I hear the subtle rustle of the sheets as Patrick moves around the bed.

Then his hands are on me again, tracing paths along my arms, down my sides, exploring with a reverence that makes my heart swell. His touch is tender, mindful of my state, yet charged with a passion that resonates deep within me.

He pauses at my belly, his kisses soft and adoring there. It's a moment of profound intimacy, acknowledging the life we've created together.

"How does this feel?" he asks, his hands roaming over my skin, igniting fires along their trail.

"Incredible," I breathe out, lost in the sensation of being both captive and deeply cherished. The blindfold heightens every touch, turning his caresses into strokes of flame across my body. I arch slightly, pressing into his hands, seeking more of his touch, more of this delicious sensation of being loved and controlled at once.

Patrick's movements are deliberate, orchestrating a symphony of sensations that dance across my nerves. I can tell he's watching my reactions, gauging my comfort and pleasure from the sounds I make, the way I shift against the bonds.

"You're so beautiful like this," he murmurs, an awe in his voice that makes me flush with warmth. "Completely open, trusting me. It's more than I could have hoped for."

The bond between us seems to strengthen in these moments, wrapped in silk and shadow. The room around us fades away, leaving only the connection that thrums through the air like electricity.

Slowly, Patrick guides my hands, still bound, above my head. The rope is secure but not restrictive, a symbol of the trust that defines the very core of our relationship. His lips find mine again, kissing me deeply, passionately, as if trying to convey all his emotions through that one connection.

Knowing I'm totally in his hands, I feel something inside me shift, a release that only his touch can bring.

He kisses me more, his lips on mine as his hand moves between my legs. He squeezes my inner thigh, tingles breaking out across my body as he touches me in the way only he can. His tongue meets mine as he spreads my folds open, his middle finger finding my clit and causing my back to instantly arch.

"There," I moan. "Touch me just like that. Don't stop."

Each slow drag of his fingertip over my clit takes me to another level of pleasure. All I can do is squirm and kiss him back as he handles me.

"You're getting close," he says. "I can tell by the way you're breathing, the way you're shaking."

I love the way he knows my body so well. But the thought stays in my mind for only a few short moments before the orgasm arrives, coursing through me, warming me, making me moan and shiver.

"You're so fucking sexy when you come," he says. "I just want to watch it again and again."

With that, he slips a finger beneath the blindfold and pulls it off. He's naked over top of me, his body as solid and sexy as ever. His cock is hard and straight, and all I want is him inside of me.

He moves down, covering my belly in more kisses, leaving no doubt how he feels about what's happening between us.

Patrick climbs on top of me, his cock pressing against the patch of hair above my pussy. We kiss, long and slow and deep. I spread my legs, guiding him into me.

When he sinks inside, filling me, stretching me, it's perfect. Patrick's body is made for mine; I'm certain of it. We kiss more as he pulls back and drives inside, another fresh, hot wave of ecstasy flowing through me.

I want to hold him, but the bindings prevent it. He presses his forehead against mine, our tongues touching, his taste washing over my palate.

"Come for me," he says, thrusting at a pace that's driving me wild. "Come for me right now."

There's no resisting him, no holding back. The orgasm erupts, and I'm arching underneath him as he pumps again and again, bringing himself to climax right as I hit mine. He fills me with his warmth, grunting hard in that deep way that I love.

Nothing else matters in these moments of pure bliss, his cock erupting inside, my walls clenching around him, gripping him tightly, making him mine.

When we're done, Patrick slowly, gently undoes the bindings, kissing, caressing, and caring for me in a way that perfectly balances the aggression of his lovemaking.

As we lay there in the aftermath, I notice that he can't take his eyes off my belly, a small smile tugging at his typically stoic face.

We're in this together and there isn't anyone I'd rather have by my side.

CHAPTER 29

ALLIE

The day stretches long and lazy, the kind you dream about but seldom get to live. I'm curled up in Patrick's study, sipping herbal tea. The dress shirt I'd snagged from his closet hangs loose over my shoulders, barely covering my panties.

It's comfy, yet I can't shake the heavy thoughts that circle like vultures overhead.

I can hear Patrick in the kitchen, flipping through his notes, the clink of a spoon against the mug as he stirs his coffee. He's going over potential restaurant specials, the scrawl of pencil on paper filling the silence.

There's something cooking, too. The constant scent of delicious food in the air is one more thing I love about Patrick's place.

I smile, imagining the furrow in his brow, that intense look he gets when he's deep in the culinary creation zone.

I should be over there, bouncing ideas off him, letting our creativity spiral into new and exciting dishes. But I stay put, my thoughts on the Mafia thing. It's causing a tight knot in my chest and demanding attention. I promised myself I'd address it before we head back to the restaurant tonight. But it's not just about confirming my suspicions anymore.

I'm in love with him, deeply, irrevocably. I'm carrying his child. Does it really matter if he has ties to the Mafia? I suppose in the grand scheme of things, it does, but it's not going to change how I feel about him. Yet, I crave transparency. I need to know who he is, all of him, especially the shadowy parts he keeps veiled.

Does he love me? I haven't gotten it spelled out in black and white yet but every look, every touch, speaks volumes. He cares, and that much is crystal clear. Maybe that's enough to build on, to create something lasting—not just for us, but for our coming child.

I set my tea down, feeling the weight of the decision I'm about to make. Confronting the Mafia topic isn't just about clearing the air; it's about setting a course for our future, determining if our foundation can handle the heavy truths.

With a deep breath, I walk toward the kitchen.

I breeze in just as Patrick is putting the final touches on what looks like a feast fit for a queen. He greets me with that killer smile that's been knocking me off my feet since day one and gestures grandly to the spread on the counter. "Voilà! For the lady: perfectly seared steak rich in iron, vibrant veggies with vitamin C, and a steamy mug of collagen broth for the baby."

I'm genuinely touched. He was diving into the world of pregnancy superfoods. My heart does a little dance—half from love, half from the sheer delight of being so thoughtfully cared for.

He chuckles as he serves me, the clink of the utensils playing background music to his next declaration.

"This baby's going to have a palate that appreciates the finer things in life, starting in the womb," he jokes, winking as he hands me a fork.

As I take my first bite, I can't help but smile, feeling spoiled and cherished. "Patrick, you're turning this baby into a gourmet before they've even entered the world," I tease back, savoring the rich flavors.

He watches me with eyes full of something warm and tender, making the veggies seem even crisper and the broth more comforting.

But as wonderful as the meal is, there's something heavy lingering in my thoughts. As we're laughing over a particularly cheesy joke he makes about baby food haute cuisine, I decide it's time to cut to the chase.

Setting down my fork with a dramatic flair, I catch his attention. "So, Chef, between prepping deluxe baby menus and running a top-notch restaurant, when do you find the time for your Mafia meetings?" I ask, half-teasing, half-serious. The air shifts, curiosity in his eyes.

"Is that what's been cooking up in your mind?" he asks, the tone cautious.

"Yeah," I admit, leaning in, the moment turning serious despite the playful banter. "I love what we have, Patrick, and I'm in this for the long haul. But I've got to know about the company you keep."

The moment is surreal, frozen like one of those scenes in a movie where you can almost hear the record scratch. The front door creaks and swings open just as Patrick and I are about to wade into some serious talk, and my heart skips a beat—not the good kind this time.

"Shit," Patrick mutters under his breath, the color draining from his face as footsteps echo through the hall.

Then, like a scene straight out of a sitcom, Caleb's voice floats into the kitchen, breezy and unsuspecting.

"Hey, Dad, the lawyer's down with the flu, so I'm back early and—"

He rounds the corner, and there it is—the jaw-drop moment. His eyes land on me, then dart to his dad, then back to me. I'm caught in mid-bite, frozen with a fork halfway to my mouth, clad in nothing but Patrick's dress shirt and my panties.

"Dad? Allie?"

Patrick stands up, a hand outstretched as if he is putting up a barrier. "Caleb, this isn't what it looks like."

I scramble to my feet, clutching the shirt a little tighter around me.

But honestly, it's exactly what it looks like, and the more we try to fabricate some innocent explanation, the sillier it sounds. Caleb's face cycles through confusion, shock, and a touch of betrayal.

He looks at me. "You and ... my dad?" His voice cracks just a bit, and it's clear he's trying to piece together a puzzle he never even knew existed.

Patrick steps forward, his voice calm but firm. "We were going to talk to you, son. It's recent, and—"

"Recent?" Caleb interrupts, an incredulous laugh escaping him as he looks around the kitchen as if it might offer some explanation or maybe an escape route.

"Yes, and it's becoming serious," I add, finding my voice because if there's ever a time to be bold, it's now. I straighten up, meeting Caleb's gaze with as much resolve as I can muster. "I care about your dad a lot, Caleb. And I care about you, too. We didn't mean for you to find out this way."

As Patrick hands me an apron, I quickly wrap it around myself. It's not ideal, but it's better than standing there in nothing but his shirt. The fabric settles around me like a shield, just in time for Caleb's next words.

"This is fucked up!" Caleb blurts out, his voice braced with hurt. "She's my ex!"

Patrick's posture stiffens, and he meets his son's gaze with a level of seriousness that pins me to the spot. "I understand this is a shock, but you need to know that what Allie and I have isn't casual. She's right—it has become serious."

I chew on my lower lip, watching the storm brew between Patrick and Caleb. There's a tense ripple in the air that's tough to ignore. When I finally gather the courage to jump into the fray, I keep my tone firm yet gentle. "Caleb, I know we dated, but it was brief and a while ago. I didn't think you'd be so upset by this."

Caleb throws his hands up, frustration washing over his features. "Maybe it didn't mean that much to you, but it did to me."

I shoot Patrick a look, hoping for some backup, but he's deep in it with Caleb. "This wasn't about sneaking around or anything shady. It just happened. Allie and I, we—"

"You just happened to fall for my ex?" Caleb interrupts, skepticism sharpening his tone.

Patrick steps in, his voice a notch softer, trying to bridge the gap. "I know it's messy. And if I could have controlled falling for Allie, believe me, I would have. But feelings don't always follow a schedule. It wasn't planned."

Caleb shakes his head, disbelief still etched across his face as he turns to me. "What was I to you, just a rung on the ladder?"

That hurt. I step up, needing to set things straight. "No way. You and I didn't work out, but it had nothing to do with your dad. You know why we split. What's going on with Patrick and me now is a whole new chapter."

The kitchen air thickens with tension. Caleb's voice cuts deeper. "How long? How long have you two been an item?"

Patrick answers though each word seems to weigh heavy on him. "A couple of months, Caleb."

"A couple of months?" Caleb's voice cracks with pain. "Great. I hope you're enjoying my spoils."

At that, Patrick's patience wears thin, his tone sharpening. "You need to watch your mouth. Don't be disrespectful. Allie isn't an object to be won."

"Oh, but you won, didn't you?" Caleb's bitterness slices through the remaining civility.

I'm caught in the middle, desperate to smooth things over but barely finding the words. "Caleb, that's really not fair—"

"Fair?" Caleb scoffs, throwing his hands up. "What's fair about any of this?"

In the heat of the moment, Patrick's control slips, and the words burst forth. "She's pregnant, Caleb. It's mine, and you will respect her."

Silence crashes down like a heavy curtain. Caleb's face drains of color as he processes the news. "You're *what?*" His voice is low, disbelief clouding his eyes.

The impact of Patrick's words hangs heavily between us. I stand frozen, watching Caleb grapple with the revelation. The moment drags into what feels like hours until he spins on his heel, his departure marked by the sharp slam of the door.

Patrick runs a hand through his hair, worry tracing his features as he turns to me, his apology clear in his gaze. "I didn't mean for it to come out like that."

I nod, though my mind races with a thousand thoughts. "We'll figure this out," I assure him, though I'm not entirely sure myself. The kitchen, once a sanctuary, now feels stark, echoing with the remnants of the confrontation.

CHAPTER 30

PATRICK

"Hey, Caleb, it's Dad. I really wish you'd pick up. I know you're upset, and you have every right to be, but we need to talk this through, son. Family is everything, and I don't want us to lose what we have. Please call me back. I love you."

I end the call and set my phone down, palming my face in exhaustion. The voicemail feels like one of many that have gone into the void.

Just as I'm rubbing the bridge of my nose, trying to chase away the headache building behind my eyes, there's a soft knock at the door.

"Come in," I call out, hoping to sound more composed than I feel.

Allie peeks her head in, her expression cautious. "Hey, got a minute?"

"Yeah, of course. What's up?" I try to sound focused, pushing my personal turmoil aside.

She hesitates, clearly picking up on my mood before getting to the point.

"It's about the menu for next week's VIP event. I was thinking about tweaking the seafood dish we talked about—adding a saffron infusion to the sauce. I thought it might elevate the dish a bit."

"That sounds good," I respond, genuinely pleased with her initiative. Saffron could add a nice touch. Run a test batch, and let's see how it meshes with the other flavors."

She nods, scribbling a note on her pad, but her next question isn't about food. "How are things with Caleb?" she ventures, her tone gentle. "Any word from him?"

I sigh, leaning back in my chair. "Actually, while I was here last night, he came by the house. Cleared out his clothes and personal stuff. Left everything else, though." My voice trails off, the reality of the situation settling in. "Haven't heard a word from him since."

Allie's face falls; there's empathy in her eyes. "I'm sorry. This is all just ... a lot."

"Yeah, it is." I rub the back of my neck. "But we'll get through it. We always do."

She steps closer, her presence comforting. "If there's anything I can do to help—"

I cut her off with a slight shake of my head. "Just keep being you. That's more than enough." I manage a small smile, appreciative of her support.

Allie leans against the doorframe, concern etched on her face. "If it would make things easier, I could step back a bit and give you and Caleb some space," she suggests, her voice tinged with unease.

I stand up quickly, closing the distance between us with determined strides. "No, that's not happening," I assert firmly, locking eyes with her. "You and the baby are part of this family now. I'm here for every step, just like I was with Caleb."

Her eyes flicker, then she nods slowly. "Okay, if you're sure. I just want to help in any way that I can."

"I know you do," I say, my tone softening as I place a reassuring hand on her shoulder. "And I appreciate it, really. Speaking of help, got everything ready for your doctor's visit tomorrow? Do you need me to do anything?"

She gives a small smile. "I'm all set, thanks. I'll need to come in late."

"Don't worry about it," I tell her, already pulling out my phone to adjust our schedules. "I'll handle it. I'm coming with you."

Her eyes light up with gratitude. "Really?"

"Absolutely," I confirm without a hint of hesitation. "I want to be there for you and our kid."

She steps closer, her arms wrapping around me in a warm embrace that I return firmly. "Thank you, Patrick. That means the world to me."

Allie pauses at the door, then dashes back with a mischievous grin to plant a quick kiss on my lips.

I reach for my phone, hitting redial for Caleb. It goes straight to voicemail again. I rub the bridge of my nose just like before, the gravity of the situation settling in.

I leave another message. "Caleb, it's Dad. Look, we need to talk, son. Please call me back."

Hanging up, I stare at the black screen. Did I push too hard? Did I make the wrong call by not being upfront about Allie and me?

The questions gnaw at me, and I stash the phone away, a heavy sigh escaping me. I'm afraid I've really fucked things up with Caleb this time.

∽

Sitting in the cramped doctor's office, surrounded by the nervous energy of young couples, I'm feeling strangely out of place. Allie is beside me, scribbling away on forms as I swallow down my internal turmoil.

"Are you okay?" she asks, peering up from the clipboard.

I chuckle. "Feels odd to be away from the kitchen during rush hour," I admit, trying to deflect my real concerns.

She gives me a sympathetic smile, her hand finding mine. "You can head back if you want. I'll be okay here."

"Not a chance," I reply, giving her hand a reassuring squeeze. My gaze drifts around the waiting room full of young, eager faces. Here I am, a man with a grown son, surrounded by couples who are likely welcoming their first child, not gearing up for a surprise encore performance in fatherhood.

Allie's voice cuts through my thoughts, her tone light but curious. "When's your birthday again?"

"April 17, 1978," I reply, watching her closely. Her eyes widen a touch, and the realization of our age difference settles in.

I can see the gears turning in her head, the sudden awareness of what it means to be having a baby with someone significantly older.

"How do you feel about that?" I ask, my voice softening.

She pauses, her expression thoughtful. Then, a warm smile spreads across her face. "I'm actually really happy to be doing this with someone who's been through it before," she admits, her sincerity shining through. "You've got the experience and the maturity. That's more than I could ask for."

Relief washes over me as I squeeze her hand in return.

Once we're called to the examining room, I follow Allie, my heart thumping in my chest. I've been through this before, decades ago, but it feels different now, more daunting.

As we settle in, the doctor arrives, brisk and professional. Allie takes her place on the exam table while I hover close by, feeling every inch the out-of-place father-to-be.

"How are we today?" the doctor asks, all smiles.

"Good, a bit nervous," Allie admits.

The doctor sets up for the ultrasound. "It's perfectly normal to feel a bit anxious," she reassures us as she preps Allie.

The doctor positions the ultrasound wand, and the room is filled with the surreal sound of a rapid heartbeat—our baby's heartbeat.

"I love you," I whisper, turning to Allie, overwhelmed by the moment.

Her eyes glisten with emotion as she whispers back, "I love you, too," and we share a kiss, sealing our bond right there in the dim light of the ultrasound room.

The doctor smiles, perhaps used to such displays of affection but respectful of our moment. "Everything looks great. Strong heartbeat, healthy development," she announces, turning the screen toward us to point out the tiny, pulsating heart.

As we look at the screen, a protective surge overcomes me, and I feel a fierce commitment to our little family.

I notice a flicker on the doctor's face and feel immediate concern.

"What is it? You said everything looks good."

Allie glances nervously between me and the doctor, squeezing my hand.

The doctor shakes her head and smiles. "Nothing is wrong. I just saw a little something extra. Here, I'll show you."

She moves the wand over Allie's belly, and I suddenly see what she's talking about. There isn't just one flicker on the screen, but two.

"What is it?" Allie asks impatiently.

"You're having twins."

The room seems to spin for a moment as reality sets in. Two heartbeats, two lives, our family instantly doubling. My overwhelming feelings of shock and joy mingle as I squeeze

Allie's hand tighter, both of us staring at the screen in total awe.

～

As we stroll through Brooklyn, the crisp air nipping at our faces, I can't help but roll out plans for the future, my words spilling out with the rush of my thoughts. "I'd really like for you to move in with me as soon as you're ready," I say, glancing her way. "We'll figure out how to announce it to the staff and set everything in motion."

She nods along, but her gaze is distant. As we walk, I delve deeper into logistics, discussing timelines and adjustments until I notice her silence.

I pause mid-stride, facing her. "I'm sorry," I admit, rubbing the back of my neck. "I get carried away with planning. It's just how I deal with things."

She offers me a small smile, her eyes meeting mine with a warmth that eases my concern slightly. "I do want to live with you, Patrick and I'm okay with being open about our relationship," she says. "But twins, motherhood ... It's a lot to process all at once."

I reach out and take her hands in mine. "I love you, Allie," I tell her earnestly. "And I promise you, I will do everything in my power to make sure you and our babies have everything you need."

Her eyes light up with the words, and she steps closer, her arms looping around my neck. "Thank you," she whispers just before our lips meet in a perfect moment of love.

CHAPTER 31

PATRICK

The weight of my phone feels heavier than usual. Caleb's name glares back at me and I stare at his number, willing myself to make the call, to bridge the gap with words that seem increasingly inadequate.

The memory of Caleb's face that day—the shock, the hurt, the raw anger—plays in a loop in my mind. It was a gut punch to see my son look at me that way. I'm torn between the urgency to reach out and the fear of pushing him further away.

But now it's different. I'm going to be a dad again. And although he's already aware of that, I need to let him know that we're having twins.

I close my eyes and take a deep breath, trying to steady the churn of emotions within. It's not just about fixing things anymore; it's about telling him he's going to be a big brother to twins. The news should be a joyous surprise, not a complication.

I should be making plans on how to support Allie through her pregnancy, preparing for our future together. Instead, I'm paralyzed by what Caleb might say or do—or not do.

I run a hand through my hair, a familiar frustration building. I've never been one to shy away from confrontation or tough decisions in my professional life, but this personal mess has me second-guessing every move I make.

My thumb hovers over the call button. For some reason, I'm more hesitant than the other times I've tried to call him.

The phone echoes through the quiet office, ringing unanswered.

Once again, it goes to voicemail, a familiar disappointment clenching in my gut. The impulse to just text Caleb the news is tempting—quick, clean, no immediate confrontation. But dropping news of his upcoming siblings via text doesn't sit right with me. It's too impersonal, too detached for something this monumental.

I set my phone down and press the heels of my hands into my eyes, thinking through my options. It's clear he's not ready to talk. He needs space, and while it grates on me to give more ground, I have to put his needs ahead of my desire to reconcile.

I get up and step to the door of the office. Leaning against the doorframe, I observe Allie in full command at the center of the kitchen. Her leadership is undeniable as she briefs the team on tonight's specials.

"Listen up, everyone! For tonight's special, we're doing grilled lamb with mint yogurt. I want the lamb on the grill now, and let's make sure that sauce is on point. I need a tasting in two minutes," she directs, her tone both firm and motivating. The kitchen springs into action, and everyone is sharply focused.

Turning to another part of the kitchen, she continues, "Miguel, how's the progress on the starters?" Her gaze locks onto the prep station where Miguel is meticulously assembling the appetizers.

"Just a few touches left, Chef," Miguel calls back, his voice respectful but eager to impress. He holds up a tray for her inspection, visibly proud of his work.

Allie examines each plate carefully, her keen eyes missing nothing. "These are beautifully done, but remember, consistency is key. Every plate that goes out should look like this one," she instructs, pointing to the plate that best exemplifies her standards.

"Understood, Chef. Thank you," Miguel responds, his smile broadening with the praise and clear direction.

A surge of pride lifts the weight from my chest. Allie's a damn powerhouse in her own right, handling the kitchen with a blend of finesse and firmness that demands respect.

That's where my focus should be—on the present, on the family we're building, and on the lives she's carrying. Caleb's issues and his acceptance of the situation will have to wait. We have immediate priorities that can't be sidelined.

My resolve firms as I push from the doorframe, deciding to join her in the fray. Tonight isn't for dwelling on what's broken but for strengthening what we're building.

I catch her eye across the room, and she shoots me a smile that could light up the darkest corners of any room. I beckon her over, needing a moment with her amidst the chaos.

"How's it going, Chef? Feeling ready to tackle the dinner rush?" I ask as she steps into the quieter sanctuary of my office.

She gives a small, confident nod. "I'm good. It's a lot, but I'm more excited than anything," she replies, a hint of exhilaration in her voice.

I can't help but throw in a tease. "I can't believe I'm about to lose another brilliant sous chef to maternity leave. What's my kitchen going to do without you?"

Her response comes with a playful glint, "Are you complaining, or just worried you'll miss me too much?"

"Complain? Never. Honestly, I couldn't be happier," I assure her, my tone deepening with sincerity. Seizing the moment, I pull her close, away from the kitchen's prying eyes. I take her face in my hands, kissing her deeply, tenderly. The kiss leaves us both a little breathless and Allie slightly dazed—a look that stirs a deeper desire in me. I want more. But her expression shifts to something more solemn.

"Have you talked to Caleb yet?" she asks, her voice tinged with concern.

Immediately, she bites her lip, regretting the intrusion. "Sorry, it's not my place to ask."

I shake my head, dismissing her apology with a firm squeeze of her hand. "No, it is your place. You're part of my family now." My voice softens. "And no, he's still not responded. Nothing."

She meets my gaze, her eyes sincere, her grip tightening reassuringly. "He'll come around, Patrick. He just needs time."

Her words, hopeful and supportive, help ease the knot of worry in my chest.

I scan the bustling kitchen, calculating the best timing for our little announcement. Drawing back into my office, I close the door with a decisive click and turn to Allie.

"We've got to strategize on breaking the news to the team," I say, my voice firm but low, aware of the thin walls. "I'm thrilled about the twins, really, but I'm not exactly excited about the potential gossip storm."

Allie flashes that daring grin of hers, shrugging off the weight of my words. "Let them talk," she challenges, her tone light but her eyes sparking with mischief.

Her boldness is a turn-on, and I'm about to kiss her when the ringing of the office phone interrupts us.

I pick it up, and the tentative but urgent voice of our hostess greets me. "Chef, there's a gentleman here to see you. He says he's an associate of Luca Amato."

I straighten up, my irritation spiking. "We're not open yet. Why is he here?" Normally, I would dismiss such an unexpected visitor, but the mention of Luca's name stops me.

I pause, taking a deep breath to temper my response. "All right, I'll be right there. Keep him comfortable," I say, keeping my voice measured and cool. I hang up, a heavy sigh escaping me as I prepare to deal with whatever this could mean.

Allie immediately notices the change in my demeanor, and her face is lined with concern. "Is everything okay?"

"Just business," I assure her, masking my annoyance. "Luca Amato's people."

Understanding with a bit of worry flickers in her eyes. She nods toward the kitchen. "I should head back anyway."

I run a hand through my hair, my thoughts racing as I prepare myself for the meeting. The more I think about it, the more I question my decision to get involved with Luca Amato. The whispers are always the same: Once you're in with the Mafia, you're never really out. They expect things, and those expectations can mold your life in ways you never intended.

With a resigned sigh, I leave the sanctuary of my office and make my way through the kitchen to the front of the house. The staff is in full swing, setting up tables and polishing glasses, the usual pre-service buzz filling the air.

I spot him as I approach the bar. He is a man who doesn't just wear a suit but defines it, exuding an air of quiet danger. His demeanor isn't loud or overt, but there's an undeniable presence about him, a calm sort of menace that seems to say he's used to being listened to and obeyed.

Steeling myself, I straighten my chef's jacket and head over. This is the bed I've made, and now I have to lie in it, but that doesn't mean I have to like it.

The man stands as I approach, offering a firm handshake that's as calculated as his gaze. "I'm Matteo Rossi," he introduces himself with a slight nod, his voice smooth and confident. "I've been looking forward to meeting the chef Luca speaks so highly of."

I nod in acknowledgment, keeping my expression neutral. "Well, you've found him. I'm Patrick Spellman. What can I do for you, Mr. Rossi?" I ask, cutting straight to the point. Time is precious, and so is clarity in these sorts of dealings.

Matteo's smile doesn't waver as he responds. "Luca was exceptionally pleased with last Tuesday's service. So much so, he'd like to book the restaurant for this coming Tuesday as well."

I raise an eyebrow, my interest piqued despite my reservations. "That soon?" I ask, already calculating the logistical adjustments needed.

"Yes," Matteo continues, his gaze steady. "He has a very important guest arriving from Sicily. Luca wants to ensure that his associate experiences the best cuisine New York has to offer. Naturally, he thought of Savor."

I pause, letting the implications of his words sink in. Luca's satisfaction could mean good business, but it also deepens the ties that I'm increasingly unsure about. Yet refusing isn't a simple option—not without consequences.

I weigh his request against the restaurant's schedule, feeling the pressure of his insistence. "I appreciate the urgency, Mr. Rossi, but we're already booked for that evening. I can't just cancel on other patrons. It would be bad for business," I state, keeping my tone authoritative yet open to negotiation.

Matteo, unflinching and clearly used to getting his way, leans forward slightly. "Mr. Amato was very clear about wanting this upcoming Tuesday. He's willing to make it substantially worth your while," he presses.

The mention of additional payment piques my interest, especially with twins now on the way, but delving in deeper with the Mafia is a dangerous path, one I'm not willing to risk the safety of my family for. My arrangement with Luca Amato was originally for one night a month. Asking for another night only a week later will most likely turn into asking for more nights throughout the month.

What have I gotten myself into?

Turning back to Matteo, I make a decision, allowing my business acumen to take over. "If I can rearrange the reservations, we'll have a deal. I'll offer them something on the house to shift to another night. But let me make myself clear, Mr. Rossi. This is a one-time occurrence. I will not adjust reservations again, not for Mr. Amato or anybody else. Got it?"

Matteo's expression shifts to one of smug satisfaction akin to a shark smelling blood in the water. "That sounds like a plan. Luca will be very pleased," he states confidently, the underlying threat clear.

I extend my hand, sealing the tentative deal with a firm shake. "I'll get on it right away and confirm with you by tomorrow."

As Matteo prepares to leave, he throws one last proposition into the mix, his voice dropping to a conspiratorial murmur. "Luca wanted you to know that he has some connections with the Michelin Guide reviewers. He believes Savor is a prime candidate for their attention."

I stiffen, my brow furrowing. "I trust you're not suggesting anything improper. We earn our accolades fairly here."

"Of course, nothing untoward," Rossi assures quickly, a sleek smile playing on his lips. "Luca would merely ensure that your talents are appropriately showcased sooner rather than later."

I exhale slowly, the lure of a Michelin Star not lost on me, but the potential strings attached regarding Luca make me wary. "Perhaps," I concede, my response noncommittal but open.

"Excellent," Rossi says, satisfaction evident. "Expect ten guests. I'll need the menu details by tomorrow to pass along to Luca." He passes me a business card with his contact information.

"Understood," I reply, my mind already racing through possible dishes that could dazzle the toughest critics. "I'll draft something and send it over."

With a final nod of approval, Rossi departs, leaving me to ponder the fine line between seizing opportunity and maintaining integrity. As the door closes behind him, the depth of the moment hangs heavily in the air.

I watch Rossi slip into a sleek black luxury car, his departure smooth and swift. As the vehicle glides away, I stand there for a moment longer, the weight of our agreement settling over me.

Running a hand through my hair, I try to shake off the unease that clings stubbornly. The money is good—great, even—and this could catapult Savor into a new realm of culinary acclaim. Yet the nagging feeling in my gut tells me I'm playing with fire.

This isn't just about me anymore.

With a deep breath, I turn toward the kitchen, the familiar clatter and bustle drawing me back to reality. As I push through the doors, the heat from the stoves and the focus of my team reorients me.

My kitchen, my restaurant, is my haven, and no one is going to change that.

CHAPTER 32

ALLIE

I'm wielding my knife with a fury, dicing vegetables at a pace that could give a food processor a run for its money.

The kitchen buzzes with the tension and excitement of the looming dinner service.

It's Tuesday again, but not just any Tuesday—this one comes with the heightened stakes of hosting an important guest from Sicily, courtesy of Luca Amato.

On the counters, dishes are laid out, looking like an edible art exhibit.

Patrick is across from me, inspecting a tray of seared scallops destined to become part of an appetizer. "These look fantastic, Allie. Make sure they get to the pass looking just like this," he instructs with a commanding tone.

"Got it, Chef," I respond with a grin, proud of the dish but even prouder that he trusts me to nail it. As I turn back to my chopping, I can't help but be thrilled with the energy of the kitchen. This is what I love—this madness, this orchestrated chaos.

As I scoop up a handful of finely chopped herbs, Patrick comes over, leaning in to check my progress. "Keep up this pace, and we might just make it through tonight without any hitches," he whispers, his voice a low rumble over the hum of the busy kitchen.

I chuckle, tossing the herbs into a mixing bowl. "When have we ever had a night without at least one hitch, Chef?"

He laughs. "A man can hope, can't he?"

He leaves a kiss on my neck, the kind that makes me forget we're in a busy kitchen for a second. Then he's off to the office, probably to deal with more of those never-ending managerial mysteries.

Once he's out of sight, my mind wanders back to our interrupted weekend chat about Mr. Amato and his merry band of suited friends.

∼

Lounging on the couch, the comfort of the evening envelops us. Patrick pops open another bottle of sparkling cider.

"You know, it won't bother me if you have a glass of the real stuff," I say, watching him fill our glasses with the fizzy substitute.

Patrick grins, and there's a hint of mischief in his eyes. "I survived this ritual when Caleb was coming along. Trust me, a few months dry won't kill me."

I raise an eyebrow, amused and secretly delighted by his commitment. "I'm impressed."

He chuckles, a sound that fills the room with warmth. "It's not heroics, just solidarity. Did it before, can do it again. Plus, it keeps me sharp," he quips, handing me a glass.

Leaning closer, I let the contentment of the moment wash over me. "Honestly, I love that you're in this with me so fully," I admit, my tone playful.

He looks at me, his smile softening. "There's no place I'd rather be," he responds, his voice low, drawing me in for a tender kiss on the forehead.

We settle into a comfortable silence, and just when I think we're about to switch topics, Patrick hits the nail on the head, like he's reading my mind.

"We never got to finish that conversation about Luca and his dinners." His voice is casual, but his eyes are sharp, cutting right to the heart of things. The man knows me too well.

I sigh, twirling a strand of my hair. "Yeah. It's kind of a big deal, don't you think?"

Patrick nods, his expression serious. "I get it, and I don't want you worrying. I'm not mixed up in anything shady. Luca likes our location and the ambiance, loves the food, and pays well for the privacy. That's all there is to it."

I raise an eyebrow, not fully convinced but appreciating his frankness. "But it's a heck of a lot more cash than a regular Tuesday night, huh? Makes a girl wonder," I quip, trying to keep it light but letting him see I'm not entirely comfortable with it.

He leans forward, his hands clasped, giving me full reassurance. "Yes, it's good money, but I've looked into it, Allie. Luca rents out other locations, too, nothing fishy. It's his way of doing discreet business. No Mafia clichés happening under our roof."

His words soothe some of my nerves, but the undercurrent of risk is still buzzing quietly. "And you're sure it's all clean? We're not going to end up in an episode of some crime drama?" I ask.

He chuckles, reaching across to squeeze my hand, a gesture filled with warmth. "Absolutely sure. It's just a lucrative business arrangement, nothing more. I wouldn't do anything to risk my restaurant or what we're building here, especially not now," he adds, giving our intertwined hands a gentle shake.

"Okay, I'll drop it. Just keep being the stand-up chef I adore, not some mobster wannabe," I say with a playful wink, easing the last bit of tension between us.

His laughter fills the room, light and genuine. "Deal. No mobster moves, just lots of Michelin-worthy meals and maybe a little kitchen drama, as long as it's the good kind."

The tension lingers, like the last note of a song hanging in the air.

Patrick notices my hesitation and nudges gently, coaxing the words out of me. "Come on, what's on your mind?" he asks, his tone soft but insistent.

I bite my lip, debating, then spill it. "It's Donnie. I overheard him at the restaurant last Tuesday night. He was talking about taking someone out," I confess, the words tasting sour as they leave my mouth.

Patrick's jaw tightens, the muscles working visibly as he processes what I've just said. "He said what?" There's a hard edge to his voice now that reassures me as much as it worries me.

"He and one of his goon friends were talking about bumping someone off or whatever the mob guy term is."

He sits still for a moment, his jaw working. No doubt he's pissed, as much as he's keeping it in check.

Finally, Patrick stands, his decision clear. "I'll talk to Luca. This isn't what Savor is about, and I won't have that kind of talk going on there. My restaurant, my rules," he declares, a definitive note in his tone.

I nod, appreciating his protectiveness, but a part of me can't help but worry about the consequences. "But what if Luca doesn't like being told what to do? What if this backfires?"

Patrick reaches out, his hand enclosing mine, his grip firm. "Hey, look at me," he says, with a warm confidence in his eyes. "I'm not about to let anything or anyone threaten what we have—not the business, not our safety, and especially not our family. I promise."

His assurance soothes my nerves a little, and I manage a small smile. "Okay, I trust you. Just be careful?"

He pulls me close, his presence a solid relief. "Always."

Startled back to reality by a quick burn with the hot pan I wasn't paying attention to; I rush to the sink to cool my hand under the faucet.

The kitchen feels eerily quiet, just the sound of running water and the distant murmur of Patrick in his office. Servers dart in and out, prepping for the evening ahead, but there's a tension in the air, like the calm before a storm.

I glance at my watch—thirty minutes until Luca Amato and his entourage descend on us again. My stomach knots up a bit at the thought, but there's something else gnawing at me, too—Caleb.

It's been over a week since he stormed out, and Patrick's attempts to reach him have gone unanswered. I haven't tried to contact him myself, partly because I'm sure he wouldn't want to hear from me, but also because I'm a little afraid of what he might say.

As I dry off my hand, I take a deep breath, trying to shake off the worry. I need to focus on the tasks at hand and on making sure everything goes smoothly this evening. But it's hard not to feel a pang of sadness, missing the connection Patrick and Caleb used to have and knowing I'm somehow to blame for the rift.

I check my watch again, steeling myself for what lies ahead. Time to get back to work, to put on the brave face of a sous chef who can handle anything—even a Mafia-tinted dinner party. But in the back of my mind, the concern for Caleb lingers, a quiet echo of the evening's anticipated tensions.

As the evening kicks off, I watch from the shadows of the kitchen as the first wave of guests rolls in. My heart does a little skip of relief—no sign of Donnie among them. I catch a glimpse of Patrick doing the charming host bit before he strides back to me with a look that says he's got the news.

"They're not all here yet," he starts, rubbing the back of his neck. "Three more on the way, and Donnie's tagging along."

The mention of Donnie has my stomach doing flips, but Patrick's quick to add, "I'll chat with Luca before his son arrives. Donnie won't be anywhere near the kitchen tonight."

"Thank you, Chef," I say, relieved.

CHAPTER 33

PATRICK

"Gentlemen," Luca begins, raising his glass in a toast as his guests mirror his action. "Tonight is not just a celebration of our ventures but a reaffirmation of our commitment to excellence—both in business and pleasure."

The first course is done; just waiting on the next. Still no sign of Donnie.

One of the guests, a distinguished man with a thick accent—probably the associate from Sicily—nods appreciatively.

"Luca, every time I come to New York, you surpass my expectations. This restaurant, this food—it's exquisite."

"Thank you, my friend," Luca replies with a gracious smile. It's my pleasure to showcase the best our city has to offer. And tonight, thanks to Chefs Patrick and Allie, we can expect something truly special."

He gestures subtly toward me, acknowledging my role without drawing too much attention.

Another guest, younger and more animated, chimes in, "Luca, you've outdone yourself."

Luca's response is smooth, his tone even. "I aim to please. And, of course, none of this would be possible without Savor's exceptional team."

As they continue to engage, discussing topics such as wine preferences and cultural anecdotes, I maintain my distance.

As the evening begins to gather pace at Savor, I steel myself for the inevitable confrontation with Luca Amato. His reputation as both a mobster and a sharp businessman precedes him, but it's the professional facade he maintains that I must navigate tonight.

Observing discreetly from the edge of the dining area, I watch Luca's interactions with his associates, noting the respect he commands and the subtle undercurrents of power at play.

Finally, I get my chance.

Waiting for a break in the conversation, I signal to Luca, requesting a moment of privacy away from prying eyes and ears. His response is measured: a nod of acknowledgment before he excuses himself with practiced ease from his group.

We move to a secluded corner of the restaurant, setting the stage for a serious conversation. I don't waste a moment and dive right into the matter at hand.

"Patrick, my friend. Is there something wrong?"

"Luca, we need to address something about your son," I begin, my tone firm. "Last time he was here, his behavior was out of line—especially toward Allie. He made her feel uncomfortable, and frankly, it's unacceptable."

Luca raises an eyebrow, his usually easygoing demeanor sharpening into focused attention. "Is that right?" he asks, the smoothness of his voice belying the seriousness of the discussion. "Tell me exactly what happened."

"Not only was he making inappropriate comments, looking at her like a piece of meat, but I also overheard talk about him taking someone out. You know I appreciate the business you bring here, Luca, but I have to draw the line. My staff's comfort and safety are my top priorities," I state.

Luca's face hardens for a moment, the affable mobster facade giving way to the shrewd businessman underneath. "Patrick, I apologize. Donnie can be ... impetuous. But you have my assurance, it won't happen again. I'll speak with him personally," Luca replies, his tone full of irritation at his son's antics.

"And I need to know that this sort of talk doesn't spill over into my restaurant. It's bad for business, and it's not the environment I want for my guests or my crew," I add.

Luca nods, a slight smile playing at the corners of his mouth, appreciating the directness. "You have my word. Donnie will be reined in. He respects strength, and you've shown plenty. We'll keep our business clean here. No more talk of the unsavory sort, and no more making your staff uncomfortable. You run a fine establishment, and I respect that," he states, extending his hand to seal the promise.

I shake his hand, feeling the weight of his assurance while also well aware of the underlying complexities of dealing with a man like Luca.

Luca's smile widens appreciatively. "I'm looking forward to the rest of the meal, Patrick. Your reputation is well deserved," he comments with genuine enthusiasm.

"I hope it exceeds your expectations," I reply, nodding respectfully before turning to head back to the kitchen. There, Allie is skillfully arranging a modern twist on a classic—beetroot carpaccio with goat cheese mousse and a walnut crumble—a vibrant and elegant dish.

She looks up as I approach, a hint of concern in her eyes that shifts to curiosity. "I saw you talking to the big man. Is everything okay?" she asks, carefully placing a delicate sprinkle of microgreens on the dish.

"Yeah, it went well. I spoke to him about Donnie. He understands the situation and assured me it won't happen again," I tell her, watching her face light up with relief.

Allie's expression softens, her earlier worry dissipating. "Thank you, Patrick. It means a lot that you stood up for me, for us," she says.

I nod, feeling a surge of protectiveness. "Always. Now, let's get these dishes out and show them what we can do."

Allie smiles but then her brow furrows with concern. "Is it really that easy? Donnie's just going to behave suddenly?"

I give a noncommittal shrug, my tone firm. "Luca gave his word. He strikes me as a man who honors his commitments. But if he doesn't keep his son in line, I won't hesitate to close our doors to them. I won't let Savor become a playground for mob antics."

I cast a glance through the service window to the dining area, noting the same group settled and no new faces.

"Looks like it might not even matter tonight. There's still no sign of Donnie."

Allie nods, absorbing my words, her expression one of relief. "Let's hope it stays that way."

As I watch Allie deftly preparing the next course, her hands moving with the confidence of a seasoned chef, I can't help but admire her. She catches my gaze, a playful smirk crossing her lips. "You know, I can't do my best work with you breathing down my neck," she teases.

I chuckle, leaning against the doorway. "Can't help it—I like watching a pro at work." Her cheeks flush with that charming blush I find irresistible.

"I need some fresh air. I'm going to step out for a bit," I say, planting a quick kiss on her cheek, feeling her warmth linger as I pull away.

Stepping outside, I breathe in the cool evening air, trying to clear my head. My mind circles back to Caleb. Still no word from him. The gravity of his silence stings. Did I push him too far? Could I have handled things better?

I'm already on edge as I walk toward the back of the building, but the loud banter and thumping bass of music only heighten my irritation. Rounding the corner, I spot a familiar, unwelcome scene—Donnie and a couple of his cronies loitering by their car, cigarette smoke swirling around them.

"Hey! No loitering back here," I call out as I approach, my voice firm.

Donnie turns, a smirk spreading across his face. "Chef Patrick! Is Allie working tonight?" he throws out casually, his tone grating on my nerves.

Ignoring his bait, I shoot back, "Your father's inside, waiting. He's going to want to talk to you." My words are pointed.

He laughs it off, clearly unfazed. "Yeah, sure, Chef," he replies with a dismissive wave of his hand.

I stiffen, my patience thinning. "And about the loitering—this is your only warning."

Undeterred, Donnie steps closer, invading my space, and deliberately blows smoke in my face. My anger flares, but I keep it under control.

"Do that again, and I'll be serving your ass for dinner," I warn, my tone turning icy.

Donnie's chuckle is dark and ominous. "You might want to be careful, Chef. The old man won't be around forever," he taunts, a veiled threat hanging between us.

With a sneer, he and his friends pile into their car and peel away, leaving a cloud of exhaust in their wake.

The tension from my standoff with Donnie clings to me as I push through the back door into Savor. Allie's orchestrating the kitchen like a seasoned pro, her focus unshaken.

I give her a wink to bolster her confidence as we continue the night's service.

I trail behind the servers into the dining area, ready to introduce the dish. But the night takes a dark turn when the front doors slam open, and there stands Donnie, flanked by his thugs.

Donnie's smug voice slices through the heightened silence of the dining room.

"Enjoying dinner, folks?" His sneer is insidious.

As his men brandish their guns, the room's atmosphere shifts from fine dining to a freeze frame of fear.

My instincts kick in, hard and fast. I dive toward Sophia, the nearest waitress. I shove her to the ground, covering her with my body as gunfire punctures the ambient music.

I press Sophia firmly to the floor, whispering, "Stay down!" My eyes scan the room, calculating my next move.

This is no random outburst. Donnie's here to make a statement, guns blazing. It's clear now—whatever leash Luca thought he had on his son has been broken. The room is a chessboard, and it's Donnie's move, bold and violent.

Shielding Sophia, my mind races to Allie. Protecting her, the restaurant, and our guests is all that matters now.

I lock eyes with Donnie, my gaze full of cold resolve. I'm ready to do whatever it takes.

This ends tonight, one way or another.

CHAPTER 34

ALLIE

Gunfire rings out, and immediately, I'm in motion.

Aiden and Sammie, two of our servers, dart past me into the kitchen for cover. My heart's racing but it's Patrick I'm worried about.

I charge out of the kitchen, my voice slicing through the noise. "Call 911!" I bark at the waitstaff scrambling around me.

Staying low, I hustle into the main dining area, where gunshots are pinging off the walls. The room has become a disaster scene straight out of a movie—chairs overturned, glasses shattered. Guests ducking and running for cover, gunmen with their weapons pointed with one outstretched hand.

Then I spot him—Patrick—down on the floor with a growing stain of red on his pants that screams trouble.

My stomach flips with fear, but I can't freeze now.

I take a split second to assess the scene—locating the shooters, the exits, and Luca and his men. Patrick's lying there bleeding, and every instinct is screaming at me to run to him, but I've got to be smart. I can't help him if I get taken out, too.

The gunfire has ceased for the moment. Breathing deep, bracing myself against the fear, I'm ready to make my move.

Across the ruined dining room, I spot Luca and his crew, standing firm and armed to the teeth. Conflict and anger etch deep lines on the older man's seasoned face.

Then, Luca's voice cuts through the chaos. "Donnie! What in God's name do you think you're doing?" His hands are out in front of him in question, trying to piece together why his son has turned a business dinner into a shootout.

Donnie, all reckless energy, smirks. "Don't you see, old man? We're just taking what's ours."

I barely register what's being said as they continue to exchange heated words. I'm too focused on Patrick. He's still on the floor, his face tight with pain, trying to keep Sophia safe.

"Allie, back to the kitchen—now!" Patrick screams despite his pain. His tone brooks no argument.

He turns to Sophia. "Go! Get behind the bar!" With a push, she scrambles behind the structure to safety. A flush of relief hits me.

But my heart stops as I am able to see Patrick's wound better. He's obviously been shot, yet I don't know the extent of the damage. I feel panic tightening its grip on me, but I have to stay focused.

"Patrick!" I yell and start toward him, my only instinct being to scream and get him out of there.

"Stay back!" he orders again, the authority in his voice mingling with a sharp grunt of pain.

I hesitate, torn. My legs are primed to sprint to him, to drag him to safety, but his commanding tone and the mayhem unfolding around me hold me back. I need to be smart.

Behind the bar, Sophia peeks out, her eyes wide with fear. I give her a nod, signaling to stay down. It's up to me to figure out our next move. Patrick needs help, but I need a plan.

Donnie and his goons crouch close to the floor, clearly trying to stage a mob-style mutiny as Donnie and Luca continue to shout at each other. It's like watching some twisted family drama unfold on TV, except I'm watching it in real time.

"Donnie, what the hell do you think you're doing?" Luca asks. His voice is cold, controlled anger spilling over each word, and his posture is commanding even under such dire circumstances.

"It's my time now, old man!" Donnie retorts, the reckless energy in his voice painting a stark contrast to his father's calm demeanor. He crouches behind a pathetic makeshift barricade of chairs, a wild grin on his face as he brandishes his weapon. "Time for new blood to lead!"

Luca shakes his head, disbelief and fury mingling in his expression. "You call *this* leadership? Turning on your family like a rabid dog and placing innocent people in danger?"

"It's the only way to show strength!" Donnie yells back. "You've gone soft, protecting outsiders more than your own!"

Luca strategizes with his men, who have barricaded themselves behind several heavy tables. As they shout back and forth, Patrick remains wounded and bleeding on the floor.

Our eyes meet, and without a word, Patrick starts dragging himself toward me, leaving a scary amount of blood behind.

"Hang tight, babe, I'm coming!" I shout, preparing to sprint to where he is to scoop him up.

"Don't even think about it!" he replies.

Two of Donnie's buddies, one after the other, stupidly pop up from behind the chairs and get shot down like ducks in a shooting gallery. Apparently, Luca has run out of patience and refuses to play ball anymore. Both men hit the ground with thuds that send a shiver down my spine.

Donnie is left alone, looking like the last kid picked for dodgeball, realizing he's out of allies, out of options, and out of time. His eyes dart around wildly before landing on me. My blood runs cold as he starts barreling my way, a determined, crazed look in his eyes.

Out of the corner of my eye, I see Patrick furiously dragging himself toward me. Each pull of his body leaves a smear of blood on the floor, painting a gruesome picture of his determination. He's shouting something, his voice raw with pain and urgency, but it's hard to make out over the ringing in my ears.

"Stay back, Donnie!" I finally hear Patrick say, his words a desperate command. But his leg is doing him no favors, and he's moving about as fast as molasses in January.

Seeing Patrick struggle, I know it's up to me to avoid falling into Donnie's grasp, but I can't seem to get my feet to move before Donnie closes the distance between us, grabs me by my hair, and yanks me to my feet.

"Come here, you little bitch," he snarls.

His grip sends a spike of pain through me, but I don't let it register on my face. He roughly shoves his gun against my temple. Across the room, Patrick somehow pulls himself up with more grit than I've ever seen, using a nearby table for support.

"Put the gun down, son. This isn't the way," Luca's voice cuts through the tension, calm but firm. He remains barricaded with his crew, their weapons aimed at Donnie but holding their fire.

One of Luca's men tries to reason with Donnie. "Think, Donnie!" he urges. "There's no walking away if you do this. Even your father can't help you then."

But Donnie's eyes grow wilder by the second. They flick around the room, calculating his slim chance of survival.

"Everyone just shut up!" Donnie snaps, his voice cracking with desperation. He tightens his grip, and his gaze makes me stop struggling. "Nobody has to get hurt if you just back off."

Patrick is edging closer now. The pain clearly written on his face is overshadowed by raw, protective anger. "Let her go, Donnie."

As the standoff continues, I can hear my heartbeat pounding in my ears. I'm locked in Donnie's uncertain grip, both of us caught up in a crazy moment that's spiraled way out of control.

CHAPTER 35

PATRICK

"Donnie, think this through, man! There's no way out of this if you hurt her!" I shout, my voice rough with pain and desperation.

With every fiber of my being screaming in anger and fear, I watch Donnie drag Allie toward the exit; his gun pressed sickeningly against her temple.

Luca shouts back at his son, his voice booming across the room. "Don't be a coward! Using a woman as a shield? Is that how I raised you?"

"Let me go, and she's free once I'm clear," Donnie bargains, his voice edgy, cornered. He's desperate, and desperate men make dangerous moves.

I grit my teeth; the idea of Allie in his clutches outside where I can't see her is unbearable. I push myself off the table, ignoring the searing pain shooting through my leg.

"Donnie, let her go now! This isn't the way to get what you want, and you know it!"

My mind races, calculating the distance, the risk. Donnie's looking at Luca, but his hold on Allie doesn't waver. He's desperate, but he's also making the biggest mistake of his life if he thinks I'm down for the count. I won't let him leave with her. Not while I still draw breath.

Gritting my teeth against the searing pain, I push forward, blood soaking through my pant leg. Luca's voice cuts through the tension, steady yet edged with a cold fury that commands attention.

"Think about what you're doing, son!" he shouts, his eyes locked on Donnie's. "This is not who you are!"

I can see that Donnie's hand is shaking slightly, the gun still pressed to Allie's head. He sneers, his voice raspy with desperation, "Let me walk out of here, and she walks, too. That's the deal."

Luca shakes his head; the disappointment etched deep in his weathered face. "You walk out by putting that gun down and releasing her. You're better than this, son. We can settle this like men, not savages."

I use their exchange to inch closer, my gaze darting between Donnie and the nearby table. There lies an unassuming weapon—a full wine bottle. It's not much, but it's enough. I lock eyes with Allie, giving her a slight nod toward the bottle. Her eyes flicker with understanding.

As Luca continues to engage Donnie, trying to peel back the layers of rage and fear that have consumed him, I move with calculated stealth.

"You think you can take over with treachery? You think that shows strength?" Luca's voice grows louder, filled with pain and disappointment. Donnie continues to look between his father and Allie, his resolve weakening.

Donnie's focus wavers, torn between his father's words and the escape he's plotting. It's a slim chance, but it's all we've got. Positioning myself just a few steps away from where Allie is being held, I prepare to make my move. The rush of adrenaline sharpens my focus—this is it, the moment to act.

In the tense standoff, my mind races for any distraction that could tip the balance in our favor. My voice booms across the room, echoing off the high ceilings, laden with a controlled urgency that I know will catch Donnie's attention.

"Donnie, listen to your father."

Donnie's head snaps back toward Luca, his eyes narrowing. The momentary lapse is all it takes. His grip on Allie slackens just enough, his attention on his father. In that split second, Allie seizes her chance.

She quickly grabs the bottle of wine, her movements agile as she swings backward, the wine bottle connecting solidly with Donnie's head, a thud echoing in the brief silence. She darts away, her movements a blur of desperation and fear.

Donnie staggers, more stunned than injured, his gaze snapping to me as his grip tightens on the gun. He swings it in my direction, and every nerve in my body tenses, knowing what I have to do. The pain in my leg is a distant echo against the drum of survival pounding in my ears.

As he points the barrel toward me, I lunge forward, closing the distance as a shot rings out, its sound muffled by the plush carpet. The bullet burrows into the floor, a mere inch from my foot.

With a grunt, I crash into Donnie, my momentum fueled by raw fury. My hand wraps around his, struggling for control of the gun in a vicious tug-of-war, muscles straining, breaths ragged.

"Donnie, enough!" My voice is a guttural snarl driven by raw anger and adrenaline. We grapple fiercely, his desperation palpable as he clings to the gun with a wild energy. But the scuffle has thrown him off balance and his movements becoming erratic and pained.

As we struggle, Donnie manages to swing the gun, striking me hard across the cheek with the butt. Pain explodes across my face; stars burst behind my closed eyes. I stagger, but the pain sharpens my focus rather than diminishing it. I channel the anger and adrenaline, twisting sharply, leveraging my body weight against his failing grip.

With a final, determined yank, I wrench the gun from his hands. The victory is short-lived as my cheek throbs insistently, but there's no time to dwell on it. I catch Donnie off guard with a swift punch, my fist connecting solidly with his jaw.

The impact sends a clear message—this is payback, for Allie, for everything.

Luca's voice cuts through, sharp and commanding. "Move in!" he orders, and his men spring into action. They're swift and efficient, pulling us apart. Donnie is pinned down by two large men, his face a mask of shock and rage as he struggles against their iron grips.

As I'm pulled back, my breaths coming in harsh gasps, I watch as Luca approaches his son, his expression a complex tapestry of anger, relief, and a father's deep-seated pain.

I stagger toward Allie, my leg screaming with each step, but relief floods me seeing her unharmed. "Are you okay?" I manage to grunt despite the sharp pain.

"Yeah, but you're not," she responds quickly, her voice laced with concern as she catches sight of the blood soaking through my pants.

"It's nothing," I insist, trying to downplay the severity as she swiftly pulls off her apron to fashion a makeshift tourniquet around my thigh. The fabric tightens, staunching the flow, her hands steady.

"Just hang on," she commands, securing the knot with a final tug.

I glance back at the remains of the gunfight in the room. Luca stands over his son, disappointment carved into every line of his face.

With a swift, resounding slap, he silences Donnie, pinning him with a look that could cut steel. "You disgrace the Amato name," Luca spits, his voice thick with contempt and sorrow. "Is this the son I raised?"

I nod to Allie, and she gives my hand a reassuring squeeze. Her voice is soft but firm. "Paramedics are on their way."

Luca approaches me, his face etched with regret. "Patrick, I'm at a loss for words. I don't know how to apologize for this madness," he starts, his voice heavy with disappointment.

I glance over at Donnie, who's being hauled off by two of Luca's men, along with the others who were shot. "What's going to happen to him and the rest of them?" I ask.

"They'll be dealt with within the family," Luca assures me, his tone firm. My son will face the consequences, severe ones. This I promise you." His gaze then drifts across the dining area's wreckage, a grimace forming as he takes in the damage.

He exhales deeply, meeting my eyes again. "Patrick, your establishment ... this shouldn't have happened here. I know you'll rebuild, and it'll be better than ever. I'll make sure of that. One of my people will contact you soon to discuss compensation for the damage."

The distant wail of police sirens cuts through the air. Luca glances toward the sound, his expression tightening. "That's my signal to leave," he says with a resigned nod.

I respond with a nod of my own, wanting him to leave.

He pauses at the threshold, turning back with a faint smile.

"Try to enjoy the rebuild, Patrick," he advises, his voice tinged with a bitter irony. "Ambitious men like us seldom get a moment's peace."

As he steps away, he adds over his shoulder, "And congratulations on the twins."

The door closes behind him, and I turn to Allie, seeing the same confusion mirrored in her eyes.

"How the hell does he know about that?" she asks.

I grimace as the reality of the ruined restaurant sinks in. The dream I built from scratch now looks like a scene straight out of a crime thriller—bullet holes pock the walls, broken furniture is strewn about, and stains darken the once pristine floor. The sight tightens something in my chest.

"Is everyone okay?" I call out to the waitstaff. They confirm they're unharmed, rising from their hiding places. Despite the devastation, that's something to be grateful for.

A sharp spasm of pain jolts through my leg. Allie's by my side in an instant, her hands gentle but insistent as she tries to ease me into a chair.

"Patrick, you need to sit down," she urges.

I nod, allowing her to guide me, but my gaze remains fixed on the devastation around us. "I don't know how we're going to come back from this," I admit.

Allie squeezes my hand. "We will," she says firmly. "We've got each other, and that's what matters right now."

Her confidence bolsters me, and I draw a deep breath, trying to see past the destruction.

The sound of sirens grows louder, and relief washes over me—Allie's safe, her face lined with worry, but she is unharmed.

Adrenaline drains from my body, and exhaustion grips me. I feel myself slipping toward unconsciousness. I fight to stay alert with thoughts of Caleb, Allie, and our unborn twins swirling in my mind.

They're my anchor, my reason to keep fighting.

As darkness edges in, I hold onto the promise of the future I need to protect. I'm not going down—not without a fight.

CHAPTER 36

PATRICK

"You're fine. You're going to be fine."

The nurse's voice is unfamiliar, far away.

As consciousness flickers, reality blends into a hazy tableau of blurred hospital scenes.

The constant in and out leaves me disoriented, barely catching glimpses of Allie's anxious face before I'm swept under again, this time for surgery. The details escape me; all that lingers is a sense of being submerged in darkness.

I come to with a start, my leg suspended in traction, swathed in bandages. My head throbs painfully in time with my pulse; each beat a grim drum of reality grounding me back to the present.

But it's the sight in the corner of the room that sharpens my focus—a man, suited, his presence filling the space with an unspoken authority. It's Matteo Rossi, Luca Amato's associate, the last person I expected to see. A chill runs down my spine at the sight of him.

Still groggy, I glance around the sterile room, half-expecting to see a nurse or Allie, but it's just me and Rossi.

"Don't hospitals have rules about visitors?" I grumble, squinting at him through the dim light.

Rossi gives a low chuckle, the sound oddly out of place in the clinical quiet of the hospital. "You'd be surprised what doors open with the right connections," he says, leaning back casually. "Luca's name carries more weight than you might think."

I don't like the sound of that. My voice is sharp, the pain in my leg fueling my impatience.

"What do you want, Rossi?"

Rossi shifts in his seat, his demeanor all business now. "First off, Luca sends his deepest apologies for the events at Savor. He's distressed about the chaos caused under his watch."

I raise an eyebrow, skeptical but listening. "Apologies are a start. What about the damage?"

"He's prepared to compensate you fully," Rossi continues, pulling a sleek pen from his jacket pocket and flipping it between his fingers—an idle gesture that belies the tension in the air. "Actually, Luca plans to write you a blank check. Whatever it costs to rebuild, consider it covered."

That catches my attention, though the throbbing in my leg reminds me to keep my cool. "Generous. And the cops? How am I supposed to keep his name out of this?"

"Handled," Rossi assures with a slight nod. "There won't be any police investigation that could cast a shadow on him or your establishment. Luca has made sure of that. Discretion is paramount, after all."

I'm not sure how I feel about that—relieved or more entangled. "And what's the catch? There's always a catch with deals this clean."

Rossi smiles, a thin, knowing smile. "No catch, Mr. Spellman. Though, think of this as an opportunity. The incident, while unfortunate, might just stir up enough intrigue to spotlight whatever you plan next. A little excitement can be quite the draw."

Leaning back, I consider his words. "So, you're saying I should turn a shootout into a selling point for my next venture?" The idea is absurd yet strangely fitting in this bizarre situation.

"Exactly," Rossi confirms. "Luca believes in your culinary art. He thinks this could be a new beginning, a story of rising from the ashes. A very compelling narrative, don't you think?"

I chuckle dryly, the pain meds making me bolder. "You make it sound like a phoenix rising, not a restaurant reopening after a mob shootout."

"Perception involves the art of painting what you want others to see," Rossi quips, standing to leave. "Think it over, Patrick. And remember, Luca is just as invested in seeing Savor succeed again as you are."

As he reaches the door, he pauses, turning back with a final nod. "Congratulations on the twins, by the way. Luca truly wishes you all the best."

With that, Rossi exits, leaving me alone with my thoughts, the pain in my leg, and a future that suddenly seems as uncertain as it is promising.

Lying back against the sterile hospital pillows, Rossi's words echo in my mind, a persistent buzz that I can't shake off.

"Whatever you plan next," he had said. It's a prompt that stirs something deep within me. Maybe he's right. Maybe it is an opportunity to start fresh with something entirely new. The thought is both liberating and daunting.

But I shove those musings to the back of my mind, my focus shifting as I press the buzzer by my bed, summoning a nurse.

I need to see Allie; everything else can wait.

The door swings open, and a young nurse steps in. "Mr. Spellman, how can I assist you?" she asks, her voice a soothing balm in the sterile room.

"I want to see my girlfriend," I say, my voice firmer than I feel. "Is she here yet?"

"She is. Been here since you arrived, in fact. I'll bring her in right now," the nurse replies with a reassuring smile.

Gratitude washes over me, followed by a pang of concern. I need to see her and make sure she's really okay. Everything else—Luca, Rossi, the future of Savor—can wait.

The nurse hesitates at the door, turning back to add, "You were very lucky, Mr. Spellman. The bullet went clean through, missing any major arteries. You should be back on your feet in about six weeks."

Six weeks. That sounds like a lifetime and a blink of an eye all at once. I nod, absorbing the information. "Thank you," I manage, my mind already racing ahead to rehabilitation, recovery, and getting back in control.

As the nurse leaves, I sink back against my pillow, my body aching but my mind restless. Six weeks to think, plan, and decide the path forward. Six weeks to heal not just physically but mentally and to rebuild what was shattered.

I'm lost in thought as the door opens again, and there stands Allie. Relief floods through me, knowing she's safe, seeing her here with me. Our eyes meet, and without a word, she crosses the room, her presence filling the space around my hospital bed with warm comfort. Everything else fades into the background; for now, it's just us.

She throws her arms around me with such force that it sends a sharp reminder of my bullet wound.

I can't help but groan—a reflex to the sudden pain.

"Sorry!" she exclaims, immediately pulling back with a look of concern etched across her face.

"It's fine," I assure her, managing a weak smile despite the discomfort. Her presence alone does more for my spirits than any painkiller could.

Her eyes search mine, earnest and full of relief at finding me awake and coherent. "How are you really?" she asks, brushing a hand gently against my arm.

"Shouldn't I be asking you that?" I reply, trying to lighten the mood. She chuckles, shaking her head. "And how's the staff?"

"Only you would end up with a gunshot wound and still be worrying about everyone else," she says with a wry smile. "I'm fine, Patrick. The staff is shaken up, but there were no other injuries. Savor, though ..." Her voice trails off, a shadow crossing her expression.

"We'll figure out Savor later," I say firmly, not wanting to spiral into that discussion just yet. Right now, focusing on us, on the immediate moment, feels far more critical. I take her hand, holding it between mine, feeling the warmth and life of her skin against my own. "I love you like mad, Allie. I'm not going to let a day go by without making sure you know that."

Her eyes soften, and a smile breaks through, mirroring my resolve. "I love you, too, Patrick. More than I can say." And with those words hanging between us, filling the space with their weight and warmth, she leans down and kisses me.

"I want you to move in with me as soon as possible," I say as the kiss breaks, my words clear and deliberate. We'd discussed the matter before, but there's a new urgency to it. "I don't want to wait another second to join our lives."

Her smile widens, lighting up her face, erasing any remnants of concern from moments before. "I can't wait," she replies, her voice filled with enthusiasm and love.

As the lingering warmth of our kiss fades, I catch a shift in Allie's expression. Her smile is gone, replaced by a somber seriousness. Something's weighing on her mind. "What's up?" I ask, my voice filled with concern.

She hesitates for a moment, and then her face lights up with cautious optimism. "Caleb is here," she reveals.

I'm taken aback, my mind racing. "Caleb? How is he?" The thought of seeing my son, especially after our last interaction, stirs emotions within me.

"He's ... it was a bit awkward at first," she admits, tucking a strand of hair behind her ear. "But I told him what happened, and he came right away. He's really worried about you."

"Can you send him in?" Allie nods, standing up with a smile that reaches her eyes. "I'll go get him right now."

"Wait," I call out just as she turns to leave. She pauses, looking back at me. I reach out, taking her hand once more. "Thank you, Allie. For everything." I mean every word, grateful not just for her support now but for being the bridge between Caleb and me.

She leans down, her lips pressing softly against mine in a kiss filled with promise and reassurance. "I'll be right back," she whispers against my lips, then turns to fetch my son.

As she leaves, I settle back against my pillows again and take a deep breath, preparing myself to face him.

Allie returns, her steps hesitant as she ushers Caleb into the room. The air thickens with a tangible tension as they exchange glances—unspoken words hanging heavy between them. Sensing the discomfort, Allie offers a small smile, murmuring about giving us space. "I'll leave you two," she says, her voice low, before slipping out, closing the door softly behind her.

The room feels smaller suddenly, just Caleb and me, the silence stretching out. He shifts on his feet and then clears his throat. "How are you holding up?" he asks, his eyes flicking briefly to my bandaged leg.

"Ah, you know, just thought I'd try out a new look for the summer," I quip, motioning toward my leg. "It's all the rage on TikTok." It's lame, I know, but it breaks the ice a little, drawing a reluctant smile from Caleb.

He relaxes slightly, finding a spot to sit at the edge of a chair. "Been staying with a friend in Queens," he explains when I probe about his whereabouts. It's vague, but it's more than I've heard in days.

The conversation edges toward the incident, Caleb's tone turning cynical. "You know, Dad, they've made dozens of movies about how dealing with the mob can be bad news. Maybe you should have watched a couple," he jests, a smirk playing at the corner of his mouth.

I can't help but laugh; the sound rougher than I intended. "Yeah, maybe a classic film or two would've clued me in," I shoot back, the humor a welcome respite from the strain.

We both chuckle, the sound welcome against the beeping of machines around us. It feels good to laugh with my son again, even if it's shadowed by the weight of recent events.

"Really though," I start, "it was supposed to be just business. Luca liked the food and liked the privacy. I never wanted any ..." My voice trails off, the reality of how quickly things spiraled out of control pressing in.

Caleb nods, his expression sobering. "I get it, Dad. It's just a lot to take in, you know?" His eyes meet mine, and there's a depth there, a new understanding.

I nod, feeling the tension in the room easing slightly. "I'm sorry, son. I never wanted things to get this messy," I confess, the raw honesty clear in my voice.

Caleb shifts, his posture relaxing as he meets my gaze again. "I know you didn't plan for any of this," he admits, his voice steadier now. "I acted out because I was hurt, but I shouldn't have disappeared. That's on me."

The air between us feels lighter, a mutual understanding taking the place of the previous chill. "Look, things are changing," I continue, my tone firm yet open. "You're going to have siblings soon. I'd really like for you to be a part of their lives."

He pauses, considering my words, then nods, a slow, deliberate motion. "I can't imagine not being around for them," he says, sincerity lacing his words. "It's going to be weird, sure, but I'm willing to make it work. For them, and for us."

Pride swells in my chest, a surge of relief flooding through me. "That means a lot. More than you know," I say, extending my arms toward him.

He steps forward, and we embrace, the hug firm and forgiving, a physical mending of the fractures between us. As we pull away, there's a smile on his face, mirrored by my own.

As Caleb glances out the window, he shakes his head. "I drove by Savor. It looks rough. What's the plan, Dad?"

"I'm not quite sure yet. Still figuring that out. Got any bright ideas?" I ask, trying to draw him into a conversation about the future.

Before he can answer, the door swings open. A pretty young doctor with dark hair and big brown eyes about Caleb's age steps in. "Mr. Spellman, I need to conduct a quick checkup," she announces, her voice firm yet friendly.

Caleb's mood visibly brightens at the sight of her, the ruins of Savor momentarily forgotten.

The doctor does a check of my vitals and declares that I need to get as much rest as I can.

As she goes to leave the room, Caleb shoots his shot. "Hey, is there anywhere good to grab a bite around here?" he asks, more perked up than I've seen him in a long time.

She laughs lightly, a sound that seems to linger in the suddenly warmer room. "Actually, the food court on the second floor isn't bad," she suggests, her eyes twinkling with a hint of amusement.

Putting on his most charming smile, Caleb asks, "Would you mind showing me the way?"

The doctor smiles and nods. "Sure. I'm about to grab some lunch myself. Follow me."

"Great, thanks. I'm Caleb, by the way."

"Amy," she replies.

Throwing me a quick smile over his shoulder, Caleb follows the pretty young doctor out of my room.

I let out a slow breath. Whatever is next for Savor, Caleb, and me feels positive, like there are fresh new beginnings just around the corner.

EPILOGUE I

PATRICK

Five months later...

As we step into the newly minted space of our Upper East Side venture, I feel a rush of anticipation. The smell of fresh construction fills the air. Allie, her pregnancy making her glow even more, waddles alongside me, her excitement tangible.

"Here's where the magic happens," I start, sweeping my hand around the state-of-the-art kitchen we've designed. There are high-end induction cooktops over there, dual combi ovens here, and this beauty," I point to a shining sous-vide machine, "is going to be your new best friend."

Allie runs her fingers along the cold stainless steel of a prep counter, her eyes alight with ideas. "Oh my God, it's perfect. I think we could shake up the comfort food menu we have planned—imagine lavender-infused fried chicken or truffle mac and cheese garnished with crispy shallots."

"It's all yours to play with. This place is a canvas for your creativity," I assure her as we move toward the dining area, where workers are adding final touches.

Stopping by the bespoke bar crafted from local oak, I gesture broadly. "And this bar will serve craft spirits to complement your dishes. Think artisan cocktails that tell a story, just like your menu."

She squeezes my hand, her smile wide. "I can't wait to see it all in action. It's going to be something special."

I pull her in close for a moment, feeling her warmth against me. "We're building something special here, baby. Together."

She leans into me, her presence a comforting weight. "Let's make sure we're ready to open these doors before these little ones decide to make their debut," she says, patting her belly with a chuckle.

We settle into the sleek chairs at the front of the place, taking in the view of New York dressed in the fiery colors of fall. Allie suddenly winces, grabbing my attention instantly.

"Is everything okay?" I ask, my tone laced with concern.

She dismisses it with a quick smile. "I'm fine, just trying to wrap my head around the fact that I'm going to be a mom to twins soon."

I take her hand, squeezing it reassuringly. "You're going to do great. Not a doubt in my mind."

She laughs softly. "Two little ones at once. Can you believe it? Anyway, I've been going through the resumes we've been getting."

As Allie fans out a handful of resumes across our makeshift workspace, her excitement is undeniable. "Check these out. I've lined up some solid candidates for front-of-house manager."

She launches into the specifics of each candidate, her energy infectious. Yet amid her enthusiasm, she flinches—another brief grimace that she tries to mask. I lean forward, my concern breaking through. "Hold up, love, are you sure you're all right? That's the third time you've made that face."

She hesitates, then flashes me a reassuring smile. "It's just the twins doing gymnastics in there, nothing to worry about."

I'm not easily convinced. "Positive? Because if you need to slow down—"

She cuts me off, her determination clear. "I'm fine, really. Now, about these resumes—"

"All right," I concede with a playful grin, letting her take the lead again. "So, who's catching your eye? What's their edge?"

Her gaze sweeps over the resumes as she picks one up, her fingers tracing the lines of experience. "This one, Sandra Whitt, has managed several high-profile spots in the city. She's got a knack for creating the perfect atmosphere, exactly what we need for a place that's going to redefine comfort food."

"You've really thought this through," I remark, my admiration for her deepening. "You're envisioning every detail, aren't you?"

She nods, her face lighting up. "Absolutely. Only the best for, well, hell, we still haven't come up with a name yet."

"We'll get there. No need to rush."

Watching her, I can't help but admire her clarity and drive. "You're incredible, you know that? This place is going to thrive, especially with you steering the ship."

"Thanks. But we'll see. This is all a first for me."

Allie delves deeper into the resumes, picking up another one that catches her interest. "Here's someone to consider—Julian Vega. He's been at the helm at The Orchard and Slate Bistro, both places known for their impeccable service and innovative approach."

But as she's speaking about Julian's accomplishments, she suddenly stops in mid-sentence, looking slightly uneasy.

"Something wrong?" I ask, my instincts on high alert, noticing the change in her demeanor.

She hesitates, a flicker of discomfort crossing her face before she forces a smile. "Uh, do you know if there's a mop around?" she inquires in an oddly casual manner.

Confused, I'm about to ask why when I notice the puddle forming under her chair. Instantly, I get it.

"Oh hell, your water just broke," I state, the reality hitting me like a freight train.

"Yeah, I'd say so," she replies with a half-grin, trying to stand up cautiously. I'm immediately at her side, supporting her as she rises.

"We need to get you to the hospital now," I declare, my voice definitive, masking the sudden surge of nerves with the confidence I'm not entirely feeling.

She nods, managing to keep her cool. "Looks like the twins are as eager as we are," she jokes.

I laugh lightly, wrapping an arm around her for support as we head toward the door.

I check my phone for the quickest route to the hospital while guiding her carefully through the restaurant. "You're doing great; just focus on breathing," I instruct, feeling a profound bond and responsibility toward her and our coming twins.

"Always the man in charge," she teases, taking careful steps.

"Only the best for my team," I shoot back with a grin, helping her into the car.

We dart through the buzzing streets of Manhattan, the city's pulse synchronizing with my own racing heart. The car's interior is filled with Allie's quick, efficient breaths as she texts Caleb and Stacy updates.

"Letting the world know?" I ask, glancing over as I dodge a particularly aggressive taxi.

"Just the VIPs," she replies with a grin, managing to look radiant despite the circumstances. Her phone chirps back with immediate responses.

Soon, we're pulling up in front of the hospital. The world seems to speed up as I rush around to her side, helping her out and into a wheelchair I snagged from the ER entrance.

"Your chariot awaits, my queen," I quip, trying to keep the mood light as I begin pushing her through the sliding doors of the emergency room.

"Very funny," she laughs, gripping the arms of the wheelchair a bit tighter as another contraction hits.

Inside, the hospital staff spring into action, taking over with practiced professionalism that leaves me momentarily sidelined. I follow close behind as they whisk Allie away to the maternity ward, my hands feeling oddly empty now that I'm no longer pushing the wheelchair.

After several tense hours, our twins finally arrive. A girl and a boy, both perfectly pink and healthy.

Allie looks exhausted but content as she holds each bundle in her arms. She smiles down at them with love shining in her eyes. "You did it, babe," I breathe out, the sight of her holding our children overwhelming every other thought.

"I had a great coach," she whispers, her tired eyes shining with love and a bit of mischief.

I lean down to kiss her, then turn my attention to the little ones in her arms. "Hey there, champ," I murmur to my son, his tiny fingers curling reflexively. "And you, princess," I say to my daughter, who responds with a sleepy yawn that tugs at my heartstrings.

"Looks like we've got ourselves a full team now," I say, straightening up and looking back at Allie.

She nods, a tear slipping down her cheek. "Team Spellman just doubled in size."

"You know, we've been so busy over the last few months that we never decided on names," I say, my voice low and filled with wonder as I take our daughter, gazing down at my tiny girl in my arms, her eyes a clear, curious blue. "Just like with the restaurant."

Allie, cradling our son, her eyes soft and thoughtful, nods slightly. "I might have a few ideas," she says, a small smile playing on her lips. "What about Shannon for her?" she suggests, her gaze drifting to our daughter.

"Shannon ..." I repeat the name, testing it out. It feels right, soft and strong. "I love it. Shannon for our girl." I look at her again, and she seems even more perfect if that's possible. "And for him?" I nod toward our son, already feeling fiercely protective of both.

Allie's smile widens. "How about Samuel? Shannon and Samuel—it sounds good together, doesn't it?"

"Samuel," I echo, feeling the name settle around him like a gentle embrace. "It's perfect. Shannon and Samuel." I laugh softly, a sound filled with disbelief and joy.

Allie laughs, too, tired but happy. "Shannon and Samuel Spellman. Our little duo."

Holding Shannon closer, I whisper to her, "Welcome to the world, Shannon. And your brother, Samuel, he's going to be right here with you." Glancing back at Allie, I add, "Just like your mom and dad."

"That's right," Allie agrees, her eyes gleaming with tears of joy. "Together."

Cradling our daughter in my arms, I'm struck by the depth of emotion welling inside me. Her big, blue eyes gaze up at me with innocent curiosity, and it's as if my entire world narrows down to the tiny face before me. I swallow hard, my throat tightening against the swell of strong feelings I hadn't anticipated.

"Don't worry, I won't tell anyone if you shed a tear or two," Allie teases from beside me, her voice gentle as she holds our son close to her.

I chuckle; the sound is a bit rough around the edges. "It might be too late for that," I admit, my laugh turning into a soft, incredulous shake of my head.

"It's a whole new chapter, isn't it?" I ask, my voice a whisper as if speaking too loudly might disturb the profound peace of the moment.

"It is," Allie agrees softly. "And it's going to be an amazing one."

As I stand by the window, basking in the quiet joy of the moment, a knock at the door pulls me from my reverie. I open it to find Caleb and Stacy on the threshold, their faces bright with excitement and anticipation.

"Hey, Dad," Caleb says, stepping into the room with a cautious smile, his eyes quickly moving to the bundles in our arms.

Stacy, ever the vibrant one, rushes in with less restraint, her voice a delighted squeal. "Oh my God, they're here! Can I see them?"

Allie laughs, then nods. "Of course, Stace," she says, her arms carefully cradling Samuel. "Meet your new godson."

I hand Shannon to Caleb, watching closely as he takes his sister with a gentleness I hadn't expected from him. It's a moment that tightens my throat, seeing him so tender, so immediately protective.

"They're beautiful," Caleb says, his voice thick with emotion as he looks down at Shannon, who blinks back with wide, curious eyes.

"Yeah, they're something, aren't they?" I manage to say, my usual composure a bit shaken by the sheer beauty of the moment.

Stacy, holding Samuel now, coos at him, making soft, silly faces that have Samuel blinking sleepily.

"They're absolutely perfect, Allie. You did good," she says, then her eyes flick up to me. "You both did."

This is what life's about—these moments of pure, unfiltered joy. Watching my son bond with his new siblings and watching Allie's best friend embrace her role as godmother, I know we're on the right path. A path that's just beginning for Shannon and Samuel Spellman under the watchful eyes of their family.

There's nothing but love in this room. And I've got no doubt that love is only going to grow.

EPILOGUE II

ALLIE

Two years later…

The morning buzzes with the kind of electric excitement you'd expect before a big opening night, only today, it's for Shannon and Samuel's second birthday party at our restaurant.

Stacy and I are in my bedroom, a hurricane of preparation as we chat and laugh, getting dolled up for the day. It feels a bit like pre-kid days, except now our conversations revolve more around nap schedules than nightclub escapades.

"Oh, please, Al," she teases, her tone playful yet pointed. "Don't pretend you haven't thought about Patrick popping the question. It's about time, isn't it?"

"I swear, between the restaurant and these two little whirlwinds, my brain has no room left for thoughts of wedding plans," I confess, attempting a somewhat sophisticated updo in front of the mirror. Stacy watches with an amused smirk, applying her mascara with practiced ease.

A laugh escapes me as I secure a hair tie. "If I have thought about it, it was while I was half asleep and dreaming! But honestly, we're swamped. The new place is booming; the kids are a handful. Where would a wedding fit into all that?"

"Just think about it," Stacy insists, her eyes twinkling as she turns to face me fully. "Patrick's basically dream husband material."

"That's true," I admit, adjusting my earrings. "He's been incredible. With the restaurant, with Shannon and Sam ... I really hit the jackpot with him."

We continue our prep, transitioning from the bedroom cluttered with beauty products to the living room overrun with last-minute party supplies that need to be taken to the restaurant.

A chime sounds on my phone. I open the text to find a picture of Patrick and the kids putting up decorations.

"Looks like the birthday duo is getting antsy," I say.

Stacy hands me my purse, a thoughtful look on her face. "You two are amazing together. He'd be crazy not to lock this down officially."

Gathering the party favors, I nod. "Maybe after today's chaos settles, we'll talk about it. Who knows? Today might be full of surprises after all."

We step out, locking the door behind us, ready to join Patrick and the twins.

As Stacy and I make our way to the restaurant, the city whizzes by in a blur of vibrant fall colors.

"Motherhood suits you, you know," Stacy comments, her voice barely rising above the music as she glances over with a smile. "You've got it all now—a booming business, adorable kids, and, let's not forget, a man who's basically a dream come true."

I laugh. "Yeah, it's pretty amazing. But now I'm wondering ... do you think Patrick's even thinking about marriage? We've never really dug deep into that conversation."

Stacy turns down the music, her expression turning thoughtful. "You two are like the power couple of the culinary world right now. Maybe he's just waiting for the right moment. I mean, Shannon and Sammy's isn't just any restaurant; it's got a star now!"

She's right. Pulling up to Shannon and Sammy's, I take in the sight of our restaurant, which has quickly become one of the city's hottest spots. Just last month, we celebrated receiving our first Michelin Star—a testament to the hard work and passion Patrick and I have poured into this place.

As we park and step out, the festive banners and balloons decorating the entrance catch the sun, making the restaurant look even more inviting. "This place is like our third baby," I muse aloud, pride swelling in my chest.

"And it's thriving, just like your actual babies," Stacy adds with a wink. "And who knows what else the day will hold?"

I chuckle, shaking my head as we go inside. "From your lips to Patrick's ears, Stacy. But today's about our twins and celebrating them. Anything else is just icing on the cake, pun intended."

As Stacy and I strut into Shannon and Sammy's, the vibe hits us like a blast of joy. Balloons, laughter, vibrant décor, servers milling about in preparation. The restaurant looks amazing.

Stacy's latest beau, Jack, an investment banker with a contagious smile, is already there. He scoops her into a whirlwind kiss, and I can't help but grin. They're cute, living that fresh, lovey-dovey phase since moving in together.

I spot Patrick across the room and, God, does he look good. He's on the floor, the quintessential dad, surrounded by a sea of toys and toddlers. The sight of him, so effortlessly wonderful with our kids, sends a warm flutter through me.

He catches my eye, that familiar grin spreading across his face, and pushes to his feet. He crosses the room in a few quick strides, the dad facade giving way to that of a loving partner as he pulls me into a tender kiss.

"You look stunning," he whispers against my lips, and I melt just a little.

No sooner have we broken apart than Shannon and Sammy barrel into us, their little legs pumping excitedly. I scoop up Sammy first, peppering his cheek with kisses, then switch to Shannon, her giggles mixing with the party's bubbly backdrop. "Happy birthday, my loves!" I exclaim, squeezing them tight.

Patrick loops an arm around my waist, his presence grounding. "They've been asking about you nonstop," he chuckles, nodding toward the kids, who are now tugging at my dress, eager for more attention.

"Mommy, look!" Shannon holds up a new toy—a shiny kitchen set that's clearly a hit. "We cook?"

"Only if you promise to make me the yummiest cake," I tease, winking at Patrick, who's already pretending to take our orders like a pro waiter.

"Two cakes!" Sammy declares, dashing off to set up his "restaurant" with his sister in tow.

Stacy and Jack join us, Stacy rolling her eyes playfully. "Looks like you've got some competition in the kitchen," she quips, nudging me.

Patrick's laugh is light and easy. "Let them start young," he says, his gaze softening as he watches our children play. Who knows? By the time they're ten, they might be running the place."

I lean into him, my heart full. "With you as their role model, I wouldn't be surprised."

"Speaking of cakes," I announce, grinning at the crowd of eager faces, "it's time for the main event!"

I sashay into the kitchen where the twin cakes I whipped up are waiting, masterpieces if I do say so myself. One is a whimsical, towering concoction of chocolate and vanilla swirls topped with a galaxy of edible stars and moons, perfect for my little dreamers.

The other is a colorful superhero-themed spectacle, complete with fondant capes and sugary masks, because who doesn't want to be a hero on their birthday?

Patrick and I light the candles, our twins' faces lighting up in delight as we carry the cakes out. The room bursts into cheers, and we all sing "Happy Birthday" at the top of our lungs, the twins clapping along, eyes wide at the small flickering flames.

After we help them blow out the candles—Shannon needing a bit of a boost to get all of hers blown out—we dive into serving slices. Laughter and chatter fill the air, the party hitting its stride.

I stand back for a moment, soaking it all in. It's still surreal to be recognized as a bit of a celeb in the New York food scene. A journalist from *The New York Times* is here, their camera clicking away. I agreed to their presence as long as they stayed back in the shadows, no interviews. I flash them my best smile, hoping I don't look as frazzled as I feel.

Just then, Luca Amato makes his appearance, his presence dominating the room instantly. Despite our complicated history, he's always had respect for Patrick, and that respect has extended to what Patrick and I have built. He clasps Patrick's hand firmly, offers me a warm nod, and then bends down to ruffle the twins' hair.

"Congrats on your success, Patrick, Allie. You've outdone yourselves," he says, looking around. He doesn't stay long, just long enough to drop off his gifts—a set of deluxe art supplies for the budding creatives, no doubt pricey and perfectly chosen.

As he leaves, I can't help but chuckle. "Only at our kids' party would New York's culinary elite and possibly the city's most notorious underground figure make an appearance," I whisper to Patrick, who gives me a look that says he's thinking the exact same thing.

The atmosphere at Shannon and Sammy's is buzzing with laughter and the clinking of glasses as family and friends celebrate. Just as the party hits its stride, Caleb and Amy walk in, looking every bit the glamorous New York couple.

"There they are! Fashionably late as always!" I call out, waving them over. Patrick, ever the gracious host, strides over with that big, warm smile of his.

"Good to see you guys," Patrick says, clapping Caleb on the shoulder and giving Amy a polite nod. "Glad you could make it."

Amy, with her sparkling eyes and easy smile, returns the greeting. "Wouldn't miss it for the world. These two munchkins are getting too big too fast!"

"We were just debating whether New York has ever seen a party thrown with such style," Caleb adds, his eyes sparkling with humor as he takes in the festive decorations and bustling guests.

Patrick laughs, shaking his head. "Only the best for my kids and my incredible lady here," he says, pulling me closer by the waist, making me blush with the pride glowing in his eyes.

Patrick's face goes serious. "It means a lot that you're here, kid. Not only today but how you've been here from the day these two were born."

Caleb smiles warmly. "Happy to do it, Dad. And happy for you both."

There's a moment where the two take a second to appreciate everything that's led up to now. Then Patrick and Caleb embrace, my heart warming at the sight.

"Anyway," says Caleb as the hug breaks. "We should say hi to the kids." They depart, Amy waving before taking Caleb's hand.

As Caleb and Amy mingle into the crowd, I lean in toward Patrick, a mischievous smirk playing on my lips. "So, when do you think those two will tie the knot? They've been practically inseparable."

Realizing what I've just said, my face heats up, and I glance up at Patrick, suddenly embarrassed. His expression softens, a thoughtful look replacing the amusement.

"Why don't we head up to the roof for a minute, get some air," he suggests, a mysterious twinkle in his eye that piques my curiosity.

Uncertain what he's up to and slightly nervous, I nod, following him as we make our way from the clamor of the party to the quiet of the rooftop.

Up on the roof, New York unfolds before us in a gorgeous panorama of twinkling lights and the golden hues of sunset. I can't help but think how perfectly the view matches the sparkle in Patrick's eyes as he turns to me, a soft smile playing on his lips.

"Isn't it beautiful up here?" he asks, his voice mingling with the hum of the city below.

"The view or the company?" I tease, bumping his shoulder gently with mine. But even as I play it cool, my heart skips a beat, sensing something big is about to unfold.

Patrick laughs, that deep, hearty sound that I love. He takes both of my hands in his, his gaze intense and full of emotion. "Both, but mostly the company," he admits, and then his tone shifts to something more serious, more heartfelt.

"You know, Allie, these past few years with you and the kids have been the best of my life. Everything we've built together, not just this restaurant, but our home, our family ... it's more than I ever dreamed of."

He pauses, and I can see him gathering his thoughts, his eyes never leaving mine. "And this place," he gestures vaguely toward the ground floor, "Shannon and Sammy's, it's thriving because we are thriving."

Then, with the city sprawling beneath us and the sky turning a fiery orange, Patrick drops to one knee, and my breath catches in my throat. He pulls out a small velvet box, flipping it open to reveal a dazzling ring that sparkles even under the fading light.

"Allie, will you marry me? Will you make me the happiest man in the world?"

Tears spring to my eyes, unexpected and warm. "Oh my God," I gasp. "Yes! Yes, a thousand times yes!"

He slides the ring on my finger, a perfect fit, then stands to pull me into a deep, passionate kiss that seals our promise. "I love you so much," he murmurs against my lips.

"I love you, too," I whisper back, feeling like my heart might burst with joy.

Hand in hand, we head back downstairs to the party, our steps light and eager. As we reenter the bustling space of Shannon and Sammy's, our friends and family turn toward us, their faces expectant.

"We're getting married!" I announce, unable to keep the giddy excitement from my voice.

The room erupts into cheers and applause, and as Patrick wraps his arm around my shoulders, pulling me close, I know that no matter what the future holds, we'll face it together, stronger and more in love than ever.

And just like that, the night becomes a celebration of not just two little birthdays but the beginning of a new chapter in our lives I can't wait to get started.

The End

Printed in Great Britain
by Amazon